# THE LURCHER

Juttal (the name means dog in Romany) belongs to an old gypsy who dies leaving Juttal to look after himself on the North Yorkshire moors. He lives very well on rabbits, sleeping in a cave near Sutton bank. Pecker, a wily poacher and expert dog handler, eventually captures him and trys to train the seven-year-old dog who has become independent of man. Juttal escapes from the poacher's home at the first opportunity and goes back to his cave to carry on the life he loves. Soon the whole countryside is on the hunt for Juttal. He has just one friend, a friend who is determined to save him from the guns.

# THE LURCHER

# The Lurcher

*by*
Frank Walker

**MAGNA PRINT BOOKS**
Long Preston, North Yorkshire,
England.

**British Library Cataloguing in Publication Data**

Walker, Frank, *1930—*
   The lurcher.—Large Print ed.
   I. Title
   823′.914(F)          PR6073.A4115

   ISBN 0-86009-572-X

First Published in Great Britain by Michael Joseph Ltd 1978

Copyright © 1978 by Frank Walker

Published in Large Print 1984 by arrangement with Michael Joseph Ltd, London and Dell Publishing Co., Inc., New York.

Photoset in Great Britain by
Dermar Phototypesetting Co., Long Preston, North Yorkshire.

Printed and bound in Great Britain by
Redwood Burn Limited, Trowbridge.

Thank you, James Herriot and Albert Gipsy Hazelhurst, for helping me with the research for this story. Without your help I would have made a lot of mistakes.

Frank Walker

Nature can be hard, raw, sometimes savage. It can never be cruel because it does not have the reasoning power. Only man has that.

# CHAPTER 1

In the cooling of the May evening the old man turned the horse on to the wide verge of the ancient drove-road. As the wheels lifted the few inches on to the grass the wooden body of the caravan creaked, the taut, striped canvas awning strained against the brackets, from inside came the clink of crockery and clank of pans; and when the horse stopped the old man sat a while in the living silence of the Hambleton Hills. In all the great travels of his long life he had seen everywhere in Britain that has a 'presence': the Gorge of Cheddar, the Falls of Aysgarth, the wild Pennine tops, the hills of Wales and glens of Scotland, but it was here, under the wide sky where the hills drop sheer to the Plain of York that Albert Lee got the 'feeling'.

Illiterate and unsociable for all of his seventy-four years, he did not have the words to express the swelling and lifting of his heart, the lightening of worn-out limbs brought by the utter peacefulness. Even the aircraft he could see slowly wheeling about the sky were noiseless as if in respect for his emotions.

Yawning, he climbed slowly to the ground and looked back along the drove-road, his brown eyes screwed against the brightness of the sinking sun. He put middle and index fingers to his lips and whistled a high shrill, three times, then he turned to the horse. A Galloway that had not been young when he bought it a Lee Gap Fair eight years earlier, it stood drooping with age and barely stirred as he took off the harness, plodding dejectedly to where the grass was lusher when he slapped its rump. He did not bother with a tether, he knew it would not stray. It was done, the horse, just like him he thought. The pair of them were ready for the knackers' yard and the horse would have to go when he picked up another, another old one for a very few pounds for he knew that soon he would have no need of horse or caravan or anything. In what time was left to him he was trying to see as much as he could of the countryside he loved, but when the time came he would have no regrets. No one could have lived a freer life than he had and freedom, to Albert Lee, was the essence of life. But the pain, when it came, was always nore intense than the time before, deeper and longer and biting further inside. The doctors might have been able to make him easier, might have been able to cure him, but he could not endure even the thought of weeks or months in hospital. He wanted to die as he had lived in his own caravan in a place he chose himself.

He was gathering stones to make a fireplace when the dog ran up to lick his hand.

'Cushty juttal,' Albert praised the dog, and the dog wagged its tail and panted.

Albert spoke English only when he had to, to his animals he spoke Romany, the language of his people. Juttal, meaning dog, was the only name Albert thought necessary for the Lurcher; he had just the one dog.

Juttal was a good specimen of that crossed breed, bred by Albert himself from a vicious Greyhound and a wily

Collie seven Lee Gap Fairs ago, and although in middle age Juttal still had the agility and speed of much younger dogs. The reason behind Lurcher breeding is to capture the speed of the Greyhound and the intelligence of the Collie in one animal and the experiment often works well. It had in Juttal's case. As fast as any Afghan, he had learned Albert's lessons quickly; not to bark when hunting, to outrun rabbits, to stalk pheasant and partridge, to leave hedgehogs alone and to guard the caravan against any strangers. Everyone other than Albert and the horse was a stranger to Juttal.

Juttal was tall at the wither, long-legged and long-bodied with a pointed face and a fawn coat of medium length which hid the bulges of muscle but not the deep, wide chest. The racing muscles were his father's the stamina and quickness to learn his mother's, his fear-lessness and occasional ferocity an accident. He might easily have been a craven coward.

Juttal lay down by the shafts of the caravan to watch his master prepare the evening meal now the cooking fire was

14

eating at the thicker twigs, the leaping flames of the gorse kindling dying down as the heavier fuel started to burn.

Albert filled the kettle from the milk churn strapped to the rear of the caravan, stood it on the stone hearth half over the fire and put a pan of stew left over from yesterday opposite. And while the meal warmed he took one of the bottles from inside the box-seat to the front wheel.

'Juttal,' he said before taking another belch-inducing swig, 'we haven't got long, me an' you. And when I've gone I don't know what'll happen to you. They'll put you down, I reckon, seein' as you'll hardly stand for anyone else tellin' you what to do,' he cackled and coughed, 'but I bet you'll give'em some stick before they knack you, eh?'

Juttal panted and licked his lips, the scent of the stew was coming stronger as it heated up. Albert gave it a stir and returned to his seat on the grass. He drank again.

'Aye, Juttal, you've been all right for a dog. In fact I've never had a better an' we've had some good times together up an' down...in fact, when we get to Lee Gap I might see it I can get someone to take you, you shouldn't have to die just because I have...there's young Bobby— or Georgie Thurnscoe. Don't you worry, I'll see you all right.'

Juttal belly-shuffled closer to the fire and the stew...The stew's main ingredient was two rabbits he had caught the previous evening on the northern edge of the hills. With onions, potatoes and sage Albert had made enough stew to feed both of them for two days and it was nearly finished. Tonight they would go after more meat.

Albert was not a thief. He was a proud man who had never taken a chicken or a lamb in his life. The domesticated fowl and every kind of cattle were bred, reared and fed by men so were their property, but he would not and could not concede that wild creatures belonged to anybody. How could they? The rabbits and hares, like the game birds, fended for themselves, found their own food, came and went as they wished and were therefore the property of the man with the skill to catch them. He knew the law

16

did not agree with him, eleven times he had been caught and fined for poaching. Eleven times he had pleaded not guilty, putting the case he truly believed, but being a gipsy had not helped him. The magistrates had heard him out impatiently, off-handedly imposed the fine and called for the next case.

He had been very careful to get his morality across to Juttal and Juttal knew better than even to bark at a sheep, cow or pig, and there were only certain times when he was allowed to take rabbits or birds. Late evening or early morning and only when Albert put on the coat with the big pockets. That old coat was the signal to Juttal, when it came from the box-seat he was all eager attention, dancing with excitement. But at the moment there was the remains of the last expedition bubbling in the pot to think about and the first things come first.

At last, when his bottle was empty, Albert started to share the stew. First he ladled Juttal's, put it out of his reach to cool and dipped the long-handled spoon again. His body arched, he dropped his plate in the fire, staggered back to the caravan convulsed in a choking spasm of coughing. He fell to his knees and hung to the wheel for support, gurgling, trying to draw breath. When the coughing did stop he sagged into the wheel with weakness, spat out blood-flecked phlegm and did not try to move. He stayed on his knees, doubled forward, clinging to the wheel. It was worse every time, more wracking, more painful, more blood. It would be soon. Juttal, torn between his master's obvious distress and his steaming bowl on the box-seat, stayed where he was.

Eventually Albert pulled himself up the wheel, standing legs astride, head bowed, trying to control his breathing so as not to start the coughing off again. Very, very slowly he pulled himself up on to the seat and sat waiting for his small strength to return and let him go to bed. Juttal moved to sit beneath him, whining a low plea. Albert grunted, 'Aye, aye,' lowering the dog's bowl over the side as far as he could reach, then dropping it. It landed right side up, spilling only a little of the thick stew and Juttal was into it, every other consideration driven from his mind. Rabbit stew formed the greater part of his diet and he knew how to get most enjoyment from it. First the vegetables and heavy liquid, then the small joints, each one lovingly crunched until the bones inside were pulverised. While Juttal was enjoying his supper Albert crawled into the caravan, dragged himself on to the bunk and lay staring, fully clothed, at the dark canvas until the last of the pain retreated and let him fall asleep.

Juttal licked the bowl clean including the outside where the stew had spilled, yawned, shook himself and went to see the horse. If the horse ever did stray too far, one bark sent him lumbering back to the camp site, but on this evening the grass close by was plentiful and Juttal could easily see him in the late twilight. Duty done, his mind turned to pleasure.

Pleasure to Juttal was moving, travelling, seeing what was round the next corner, beyond the next gate and it was his habit when Albert had retired to make a tour of the district.

Here, on the southern edge of the Hambletons, the ground ran fairly flat

19

from the drove-road to the escarpment where some prehistoric upheaval had fractured the earth's crust leaving a five hundred foot drop from the hills to the plain. Not a vertical bare cliff but a jumble of varying slopes, some with lesser slopes or small precipices all well-covered by greenery, trees, bushes, grasses and seasonal flowers. A natural place spoiled only by the narrow twisting road which climbed Sutton Bank further to the south.

Each year Albert had made his camp on the drove-road and Juttal knew the area and liked the escarpment. Nowhere else on their journeying was there anything like it and he set off to the west, deviating only to make a wide swing round a farm, the picking up his course again. It was not far for his legs and when he got there, at the very edge with the endless patchwork fields spreading away down the length of England, a white three-quarter moon was silvering the scene.

A human would have been awed at the grandeur, reduced to the realisation of his insignificance, but to Juttal there was only the pleasure of visiting an old haunt, which is the ultimate joy of travelling. He would not have wearied of the escarpment if Albert had decided to make a permanent home there, nevertheless he would be ready to move on whenever Albert started to harness the horse. The strengthening moonlight was a help, not to use to admire the black blocks of the farms or the haphazard lines of the hedgerows so far below, but to pick his way down the first slopes to a bush which was emitting a faint rustling that would stand investigation.

This first short slope was steep, Juttal had to slide and scramble and whatever had been making the noise in the bush had gone when he got there. No matter, there were lots more bushes and he knew this place abounded with small animal life, there would be some chasing to do.

Not being hungry he had no inclination to hunt for the sake of killing. He would chase anything that moved and kill it if he made a capture for that was the instinct of his father, but without Albert to order him he would not hunt for food with tomorrow in mind. His

21

belly was full. When it was empty would be time enough to get serious.

Down he went on a zigzag course, the fullness of his belly ruling out the need for stealth, simply taking the easiest way and seeing what he could see. The nocturnal hunters were active. He saw an owl pounce, the glimpse of a brush as a fox made way for him, then two small luminous green discs and the scent telling him here was his mortal enemy, a domesticated cat from one of the farms. Hunting did not enter into this, nor the sheer love of the chase, this was the age-old cat and dog feud and Juttal accelerated across the moonlit slope to put an end to the hated feline. The cat was fast also, the shining eyes vanishing as it turned to run for its life to the nearest tree. The streaking black shape reached the first thick trunk five yards in front of Juttal and when Juttal skidded to a stop the cat was looking down from a fork well out of reach. Juttal walked round the tree, puzzled as he always was by the way cats could get to where he could not follow. For a few minutes he prowled threateningly, looking up and growling and knowing from past chases the cat would stay up there as long as it could see him. Juttal lost interest in the cat. He went on his way down the escarpment.

He was aware all the time of the life above him, around him and below him, reading the tiniest rustling, the thumping of rabbits running for cover, and taking no conscious notice. He could see the moon reflecting on the water and made for the lake. Once he had caught a migrant mallard on the side of the lake and Albert had praised him for a long time. The duck and the fish Albert had taken had made a feast when they camped at a safe distance the following evening.

It was very peaceful down by the lake where Juttal drank, the moon shining from deep down in the still water, the insects chirping and whirring, the sly movements murmuring in the undergrowth. But Juttal was not human and all that ghostly beauty was lost on him.

Until very late he roamed the face of the escarpment, visiting a small cave where some foxes had once lived, but the foxes had moved—or had been moved— and there were only old scents, nothing to excite or hold the attention.

He lay down and rested a few minutes outside the cave which was behind a heap of rocks beneath a small rocky overhang. Two hundred feet above the plain, half a mile from the road to the south, he could see the lake glinting blackly now the moon had passed, the village of Sutton with a few lights, the chequer of fields with the spaced-out farms receding into the silvery darkness to the west. Far away from the west, came the clear thrumming tremor of heavy vehicles on the A1.

Juttal yawned, got up, shook vigorously, started the steep climb back to the caravan. Much as he liked the lonely quiet places, habit told him to return to sleep close to his master; habit, the unbreakable chain that ruled his life. The horse slept on as Juttal went quietly under the caravan where he slept and Albert's snores said that everything was in order. Juttal flicked up his tail to cover his nose and fell immediately into the heavy sleep of the justly weary.

The first song bird woke him, and he

24

came from total unconsciousness to his full senses in the time it took for his eyes to open. He did not move. Long ago when he was still a pup and had to be tied to the wheel at nights, he had learned that it was wrong to start living the day until Albert came yawning to the door. Albert did not like dogs that barked for joy at the first light of day, he liked dogs which lay silently under the caravan until told to come out. Unless there was a warning to give and then Albert liked dogs with a bark furious enough to drive off any possible intruder. Barking was not to be considered a frivolous exercise, it was a weapon, the first line of defence, and must be used prudently.

So Juttal lay watching the pink and orange of the sunrise shading into the blue of promise, the promise of another perfect spring day. Somewhere to the north the lambs were bleating plaintively or crossly as they waited for tardy mothers to provide breakfast and further away still an angry cow bellowed. He heard, from near the escarpment, the last scream of an unwary rabbit. Each sound was a picture in itself and would have sped by a human ear unheeded but Juttal heard it all and much more. There were flapping wings and whirring wings, piping songs, desultory squawks and caws and faintest of all the angry scream of an invisible gull. Everywhere on the plateau, back in the hills and down the escarpment, life was being lived at the precarious pace of the wild. The young of all species were growing and gaining strength, the survivors learning to evade the predators, the predators using more cunning to outwit increasing knowledge and speed, but speed and wit which would never develop to a degree that would upset the balance of nature. Only the fastest prey would live just as only the craftiest of hunters would eat.

That morning Albert was very late in rising, two hours after the sun and far too late to go looking for meat. The countryside would be crawling with farmers and shepherds at that hour, not that Albert gave any thought to food. The pain was inside him again, taking his strength, and he came very slowly down from the caravan. He held on to the side with his breath rasping, trying to

26

summon enough energy to light the fire and make tea and when he let go he swayed, nearly fell, grabbed at the wheel. Heaving up the lid of the box-seat, he took out a handful of twigs and sticks, tossed them near the fireplace, felt for the tea and sugar tins, lowered himself to the ground and crawled to the cold fire.

Pitifully—critically—ill as he was, it was the work of seconds to get the blaze going. He shook the black kettle and sighed when enough water sloshed about, put the kettle over the flames and slumped to his elbow to watch it boil. He had forgotten his tin cup. He used up a lot of curses crawling the few yards to the caravan and back as he waited for the kettle to sing.

With his milkless tea brewing in the cup he crawled to sit on the ground with his back to the wheel. Juttal came to lie beside him, upturned eyes fixed on his master's drawn face. Albert sucked noisily at the hot drink and put a hand on Juttal's head, 'It's going to be sooner than I thought, Juttal. The old gry looks close, as well.' Gry was his Romany word for the horse, which was awake and standing in its usual dejection, as worn as Albert and not even bothering to walk the few yards to where the grass was long and sweet.

All three stayed in the same position until long after Albert had drunk his tea, Albert and the horse because they had neither the strength nor the will to move and Juttal because he was content. Soon Albert would get up to harness the horse and they would be off again to the south to some other old favourite camp site.

But for once it was not like that. When Albert did drag himself up he pulled himself into the caravan and Juttal heard the bunk creak. It was very puzzling. The only time they spent more that one night at a camp was at the fairs and this old drove-road was not a fair. Juttal made his protest by jumping on to the box-seat, putting his head into the dimness and barking.

'We're stoppin' here today,' came Albert's voice.

Juttal barked again.

'I said we're stoppin' here. Take yourself off for a bit.'

Juttal barked.

28

'I said,' there was a sound of scuffling, 'take yourself off!' An old boot came from the dark , not with any great force, but it clipped Juttal's muzzle and if he could not understand what Albert said he knew from the past what a thrown boot meant. He jumped to the ground and was immediately on the alert. Approaching from the south was the sound of a noisy vehicle and after a short time a tractor came over a rise. Juttal went to the edge of the verge to place himself between the tractor and the caravan and waited with partly-bared teeth.

It was an open Fordson driven by a curly-headed youth with the brown face of a countryman. The closer the tractor came the higher Juttal's upper lip curved at the threat; when the boy was level with the caravan only the noise of the engine hid the menacing snarl. The boy sensed it and wisely said nothing. Boy and dog regarded each other, the boy with suspicion tinged with fear and Juttal with unmasked hatred. The youth's tense shoulders relaxed visibly when the dog let him by unscathed and he hoped heartily the caravan would have moved on when he came back in the evening. Juttal stayed on guard until the tractor had turned into a distant field and sounded no louder than the buzz of a bee.

Juttal took a turn round the camp. The horse had moved to the better grass and was cropping half-heartedly, Juttal had staved off the intruder, the camp was in good order so there was no need to hang about. He set off for another place that he remembered.

Alan Barnes brought the empty buckets from the pigsty. He walked quickly to the back door of the old stone house, scattering free-ranging chickens and ducks, left the buckets by the outside tap and went in for breakfast.

This time last year he had been affable, spreading his quick wit and laughing a lot. The lambing had been good and the overdraft diminishing, the farm and finances showing materially the five years of effort to pull the farm back from the brink to which his father had let it slip. Run down, old fashioned, almost bankrupt, the place had nearly been

30

ready for the hammer when Harry Barnes' death had brought Alan home to Yorkshire from the Canadian wheat belt. After working for the progressive North American farmers Alan was ready to give up in despair at the first sight of Lane End farm—his first sight for eight years. Only the pathetic persuasion of his overworked mother had kept him there.

At first he had felt shut in even out in the open after living in the vast prairie land, but that illusion had gone, along with his misgivings, when he put his back into the rescue job.

The first two years, naturally, were the hardest. First he had built the modern concrete pigsties himself, then demolished the old ones and built a new wooden byre on that site. Then the old byre had come down and up had gone a garage for the vehicles. The chicken houses he had got away with repairing and his smiling banker—who had a tendency to scowl in Harry's day—had advanced the money for Alan to lease two more fields to expand the flock. Deeply but not unhappily in debt he had started on wiping out the overdraft and

31

then last summer the disasters had begun to happen. New fuel injection for both tractors was followed by the byre with the herd in the night, catching fire and burning down. How that happened was still a mystery. The most logical explanation was a cigarette end dropped by the herdsman, Archie Rowe. Archie denied it and even if he had not it made no difference. A new byre had to be built. It was not so much the byre as the dairy herd it cost and, foolish though it was, Alan had been a long way under-insured.

The bank manager had been stern. It had taken him two weeks to decide Alan was worth another chance and the overdraft had been extended to the limit of the total value of the farm: the land, the buildings and everything on it or in them. If he tripped again, Lane End would be hearing the cry of the auctioneer.

A bad winter necessitating costly feed for the sheep had been followed by an almost disastrous lambing and now it was touch and go again. And pigs were not what they were, with the government bowing to the wishes of the Common Market and taking away the vital subsidy. The blue sky of his life had changed to thunderous grey and this year, with whatever result it brought, could not end quickly enough for Alan Barnes.

His worries, however did not stop his mouth watering at the smell of frying bacon and eggs. His mother took two eggs from the pan and cracked in two more.

'It won't be a minute,' she said without looking up, 'is Archie coming?'

'He shouldn't be long.'

Alan was always twelve hours behind with the newspapers; he spread a copy of the *Evening Post* on the large table and tried to lose himself in the glory of Leeds United.

Deftly Alice Barnes basted the eggs, put them on the heaped tray in the oven and cracked in the last one for herself.

She was sixty-two and with a kinder life would have looked under fifty. The bitter lines drawn around her mouth by the years of hopeless frustration were still there, too deep to be erased. She would never have admitted it to anyone but she had been happier since the death of her husband and the return of Alan than at any time in her life except when she had been blinded by her one short-lived romance. Harry Barnes had been good-looking, considered *the* prize amongst the girls, and Alice's common sense had flown when he started courting her. It had returned with a sickening thump six months after she came to live at Lane End when she realised that all Harry wanted was a housekeeper on the cheap. Her husband was a philanderer and, for a farmer, a wastrel but in the mid-thirties old values still existed and it never entered her head to desert him. And there was her coming baby to think about and provide for.

She put the heaped tray on the table and went to the door. 'Archie! Your egg'll be hard again!'

Archie came from the byre and waved. Alice poured the tea as Alan helped himself to bacon, sausage, kidney, mushrooms and eggs.

'Are you going into Thirsk today!'

She nodded. 'As soon as I've cleared up. I want to get the shopping done

34

before the race crowds start to arrive.'

'You can drop me off at the club, then, I'll have to have a break today.'

Reduced to one small car they had to plan its use. Alice took almost as much food as her son and said earnestly, 'I keep telling you, you should take more time off. You won't do much good working yourself to death.'

'Mornin' all!'

Whatever catastrophe happened at Lane End there was always one cheerful face. Archie Rowe clumped across the flagged floor and dropped grinning into his chair. All he expected from life were forty Woodbines, somewhere in the region of ten pints of beer each day and a couple of pounds to back the racing certainties he selected on Saturdays. Clothes he did not even think about, and if Alice had not from time to time bought new ones before giving him his wage the ones he had would have disintegrated on his body. He did not mind the liberty she took with his money, he never seemed to mind anything.

'Anyone want owt else?' he grinned with the tray poised over his plate. When they both shook their heads he transferred the remaining food to his plate with one sweep of his knife. He was forty-two, a year older than Alan, and had worked at Lane End since leaving school. His mind was uncomplicated, uncovetous and mostly for those reasons he was a happy man. Once each week on his day off he would put on his best clothes and take off on his old 250cc motor bike. Where he went he would never say and when teased by Alice about the lipstick on his handkerchief he simply grinned and winked.

'Y' know what?' he started the breakfast conversation with his usual preliminary.

Alan gave up trying to read the paper, 'What?'

'Y' ought to think on what I said about 'osses. They had a programme about 'em on the telly last night. Shires an' Clydesdales. Beat tractors any time an' y'd save thousands i' t'long run.'

'Just now we'll have to make do with what we've got. I couldn't afford a Shetland pony, never mind a cart horse.'

'Aye,' Archie went on unheeding,

'no diesel, no mechanics' fancy prices, no brekkin' down...'

When Alan had eaten and smoked his first cigarette to the background drone of Archie's argument for the return to true horse power, he took the powerful field-glasses from the hook behind the door and stood leaning in the doorway with the glasses trained on the upward sweep of hill behind the pigsty. He found the scattering of white dots that were his flock and picked out his shepherd, Mannie Fairbrother. Mannie was twenty-eight years old with twenty twenty vision and he raised his crook in the signal that all was well with himself and the sheep. Mannie was a good shepherd. He lived with his teenage wife in the tied cottage at the foot of the grazing land, with no electricity, no running water, heat and light from Calor Gas containers and the television powered by battery. Neither of them showed any desire to move into a more modern way of living. With generations of farmers behind them they would have been lost away from the only environment they had known.

Alice was washing the dishes when

Alan hung up the glasses.

'We'll be back about dinner time,' he told Archie as the herdman was going back to his cattle. 'Look out for Jim, he'll be coming to see that heifer's hoof's all right—and don't forget to give him a drink.'

'I'll do that,' Archie grinned. The vet, a true Scot, liked a glass of whisky and insisted on the host joining him. All his years in England had robbed him of neither his accent nor his love of 'barley water'.

Alan brought the car from the barn, sitting waiting with the engine running to hurry Alice up. She came out clucking her tongue and pulling on her coat, 'You know I don't like being rushed, there's plenty of time.'

He let in the clutch as she pulled the door closed, 'I want to be first on the list, there'll be a lot there on a day like this.'

It was a drive of seven miles that would have been covered in as many minutes on a motorway. Through the twisting, rolling lanes the journey took a little more than twenty minutes. Alan watched his mother drive slowly back down the bumpy, unmade lane, took a look at the wind sock and went into the office to book his launching.

The Yorkshire Gliding Club has its home on top of the escarpment, the wide field running to the very edge of a sheer drop of hundreds of feet. The cliff is the western boundary. To the east the air is made turbulent by thick woods and it is necessary for experienced pilots from other clubs to learn the peculiarities of being launched from an escarpment top.

Alan had learned to pilot a glider before going to Canada and had picked up the sport again as soon as he returned. For a man with his living literally in the soil it was perfect relaxation to sail far above the fields in a cocoon of peace disturbed by nothing more than the rush of the wind.

It was ten minutes past nine and he was the first flyer of the day into the office. The Chief Flying Instructor, Stanley Marsden, was opening the mail and waved for Alan to come around the counter and take a seat. They were old friends, Stanley had taught Alan how to fly and was now getting close to retiring age.

'I won't be long, put the kettle on, I haven't had a drink yet.'

Alan filled and plugged in the kettle, hunted for tea bags and milk. 'It's the middle of the afternoon, mate, good job you're not a farmer.'

Stanley grunted and ripped open another envelope. He stacked the letters and enclosed cheques, sipped his tea with eyes closed in ecstasy, 'Aaahh. Where've you been keeping yourself, must be over a month since we saw you?'

Alan sat on the edge of the desk. 'Busy, it's all go trying to pull the farm out of the mire. I'll do it, though.'

'You will, but it's no good killing yourself in the attempt.'

'You sound like my mother.'

'She's right. All work and all that'

Alan went to the window for a look at the wind sock. 'It's good today, seven or eight knots and warm enough for a thermal or two.'

A glider's means of power is gravity. After being towed or winched aloft the flying is a steady descent toward the pull of the earth and at the correct angle the airspeed will be about 42 knots. To climb, the pilot searches for thermals which are either columns of rising warm air or an updraught such as is caused by a westerly wind hitting the face of the escarpment.

Alan signed the statutory form, paid £3.30 for an aerotow to a height of 2,000 ft, and went out to get his name first on the list.

It was 9.20 and other members were arriving and coming from the club caravan park. Miles Thompson, pilot for that day of the Piper Cub, held up a thumb as he climbed in to start warming up the machine and at dead on half-past Alan helped to push back the hangar doors and manhandle a single seater club glider across the field to the take-off point. He was a member of a six man syndicate which owned a private glider but the club machines held preference over those privately owned in order of launching and that morning he did not feel like queueing. The club machines were imported from Czechoslovakia as there were no British-built craft at a comparable price and the metal skin flashed silver in the sunlight. To Alan the flowing aerodynamic lines of the little engineless craft represented true beauty. The thrill of the imminent prospect of sailing the skies, turning all the power of nature to his own advantage, meeting and beating the challenge of suddenly changing conditions, had not palled for him and he smiled as he climbed into the tight cockpit, fastened the safety harness and waited for Miles to taxi across and take him off the ground.

He made the pre-flight checks to see that the controls were working properly and easily, positioned the elevator trim, pulled and pushed the release knob for the towing cable and was ready.

The Piper Cub engine crescendoed and Miles brought it steadily into position ahead of Alan. Another senior club member who was in charge of launching for that day clipped the towing hook into the nose. Alan pushed home the knob to secure it, someone else swung over the perspex hood and Alan raised a hand to show he was ready. A pupil pilot held the glider level by the starboard wing tip and Miles inched the Cub ahead until the cable was taut and Alan had the first thrill of living movement when the glider's single wheel started to bump over the grass.

Miles steadily opened the throttle, the bumpy progress of the glider became a quickly thudding rumble, the youth at the wing tip ran with them as far as he could and by then the glider had enough speed to maintain its own balance. Acceleration was rapid then and when the air speed indicator read 34 knots the rapid bouncing stopped and Alan was airborne. Seconds later the Cub's undercarriage left the ground and they were climbing to clear the trees to the east. With a feather touch on the control column and rudder bar he kept the correct line of flight behind the Cub and the altimeter climbed to the 2,000 ft he had paid for. A double pull on the release knob to make sure the hook fell clear and the Cub was banking and turning to starboard to return and launch the next customer. And Alan was where he wanted to be with the wind hissing by at 42 knots and all the sky to play in.

Glider navigation is largely by landmark and on his north easterly heading he could pick out the tiny communities, Cold Kirby, Scawton, Old Byland, Boltby. He knew where to look far ahead, to where Lane End farm and all its problems lay waiting for him. He banked away from the farm more to the east and at once hit a thermal. Quickly he gained height to 3,000 ft and increased his angle of attack, pushing his speed up to 55 knots as he tried to leave the farm with its worries behind. He wanted to find another thermal that would lift him high enough for aerobatics. He needed the exhilaration.

# CHAPTER 2

The copse was dense, the light dimly grey-brown in contrast with the sunlight outside. The sun pierced the foliage wherever the branch canopy left a gap, the golden shafts lighting up the dank undergrowth. The pale blonde shadow that was Juttal moved on a noiseless, twisting path through the close-growing trunks.

Twelve months earlier the Lurcher had found a nest in a brush-covered gully, a nest containing thirteen eggs and unguarded. Juttal had broken and eaten the eggs, leaving a pitiful mess of demolition for the mother bird to return to.

Taking eggs was not stealing, for eggs did not move, try to fight for their lives, or simply run for cover. They were not in the vicinity of farm buildings nor under the care of sheepdogs. Therefore they were legitimate prey to be enjoyed as a passing snack. Juttal was searching for eggs again but this time his luck was bad. He was too late; the three nests he found held only shell fragments and the chicks that had broken out of them were already gaining strength on the wing.

He did find a pond and tried to catch one of the squat, leaping creatures but they were too quick for him, diving neatly under the floating leaves at the sound of him forcing his way through the tall ferns.

Juttal did not particularly mind the fruitless journey—it was not exactly fruitless. He had followed several clear, well-used rabbit runs and would remember the heavily populated burrows He drank at the pond and went on his way, leaving the copse where it met the slope of a hill. As soon as he was out in the open he stopped still, wary, hackles lifting a fraction. Scattered across the hill was a flock of sheep and watching the sheep was a man with two dogs.

The dogs were black and white Border Collies, one an old hand, the other young enough to be a probationer, and it was the young one that saw Juttal on the edge of the trees. It barked its challenge and Juttal held his ground.

The man waved his crook, yelling: 'Bugger off, now,' not wanting his brainless charges scattered by the smell of a strange dog.

The words were gibberish to the Lurcher but the tone of voice and shaking of the crook were unmistakable. Owned by a gipsy, being moved on by various people in authority was part and parcel of living, something which happened almost weekly, and although he would have fought with the dog he did not consider defying the man. He turned and went back through the copse.

He had travelled a long way after leaving the caravan that morning, the sun was more than halfway down to the horizon and he was getting hungry. His nose pointed unerringly homeward when he came out of the trees and he stepped his pace up to a fast lope, skimming across field after field and showing the characteristic inherited from his father; graceful, untiring leg power.

He leapt the stone wall on to the drove-road, his paws kicking up puffs of the loose white surface, and saw that the horse had strayed. It had methodically cropped its way along the roadside and was a quarter of a mile away beyond the caravan. Juttal shot past the caravan and performed one of his few duties in rounding up the horse. The horse knew what the bark meant, plodding slowly back after the dog who had gone to see what was doing in the food line. There was nothing doing. The ashes were cold in the fireplace and Albert was still in the caravan. Juttal made sure the horse was close enough and lay down under the caravan to rest and wait.

Time had little meaning for Juttal. His life was regulated by daylight and darkness, harnessing and unharnessing the horse, and eating. All Juttal had to do was wait for Albert to come out to cook dinner, enjoy his meal and then please himself whether he snoozed by the fire or under the caravan, or went on a sight-seeing tour.

Today's roaming had tired Juttal more than he knew. He lay with his chin on his

48

paws watching the horse and then he was waking up in the dark. Some high cloud drifting in from the east had covered the moon but there was enough starlight for Juttal. The horse was still there sleeping and Albert was still in the caravan. It was then that Juttal became uneasy.

In a way of life ordered by habit there were certain things to do when certain occasions arose, such as bringing back the horse and not falling too far behind the caravan, always being at the camp site when the sun came up so as not to keep Albert waiting if he wanted to make an early start, but this situation was a new one and Juttal could not reason what action to take. All he could do was wait and the increasing hunger made waiting very irksome.

Juttal waited and waited and the horse slept and there were only the night-time country sounds. No food. When the clouds covered all the sky and the rain started he went under the caravan and slept.

He was awake before the sun, before the false dawn started to grey the eastern sky. Above him there were no creakings

of Albert moving, no loud, open-mouth-
ed breathing. Juttal could only lie there
on his aching belly and wait for he knew
not what.

All about him the night creatures lived
their lives. Somewhere back along the
road a badger trundled along snuffling
and grunting. Towards the escarpment
an owl-hoot was answered and on the
breeze that was blowing away the rain
clouds came the whiff of a fox. It is in the
secret night that nature is most active.

But Juttal was not nocturnal and he
dozed on, coming alert at each new
sound, until the upper rim of the sun
climbed over the hills promising to dry
out the earth and provide a warm,
pleasant day.

He came out from his sleeping place
for his first shake of the day. He relieved
himself against a wheel and eyed the
horse which was fifty yards away
drinking from a puddle. That was all
right. He made a search of the ground
under the box-seat looking for scraps
and was out of luck there.

He heard a vehicle coming and ran
round to take up his guard duty. It was

the youth driving the tractor again and this time he tried to make friends. He got no encouragement.

'Now then, lad,' he called over his roaring engine as he drew level. Juttal raised his upper lip a fraction more and when the boy smiled, 'What's up, then?' he made their relationship—or lack of it —clear with a short bark and a long snarl. The boy roared and rattled away, glad he was aboard his machine and not on foot.

The morning dragged with nothing to do but wait. Twice the horse had to be brought back but apart from that Juttal lazed in the sunshine. The day was beautiful, with a few creeping white clouds and swooping, whizzing swallows back from the Mediterranean. The bees were dancing about in the small blossoms and from three directions Juttal could hear the querulous lambs.

It was about noon when the first faint foreign noise woke him from a doze induced by boredom. His ears went up and he listened. It was there again and fractionally nearer, the drone of a monotonous voice. Juttal was fast

51

coming from under the caravan to the road side. Approaching him spread right across the width of the road and verge was a party of children out for a nature lesson. The teacher was middle-aged and bored with the years of trying to get children interested in the glory of the countryside. His lecture was a recital perfected and he could have reeled it off in his monotone at any given minute.

'...and this very road you're walking on is part of the National Heritage. Until the railways came the drovers brought cattle along these roads in their hundreds and thousands, all the way from the Highlands to Smithfield market in London. Three thousand head sometimes, all shod like horses and driven by the drover, two or three whippers-in and a dog. The whippers-in were—ah, there's a dog now, not a drover's dog but a dog that uses the roads by the look of it. A gipsy's dog and I haven't seen a caravan like that for years. Now—'

'Please, sir—'

'Silence when I'm speaking. As I was saying—'

'Please, sir.'

The party was now about thirty yards from the camp with Juttal standing, hackles on the rise, close by the roadside. The teacher paused to look at his questioner who was at the rear. 'Well?'

The child was eleven years old and the whiner of the class, 'I don't like dogs.'

'For how long,' the teacher asked of the stratosphere, 'am I to be persecuted with Simpsons? Year after year, without fail, there is a Simpson delivered to plague me. Do your parents hate me, Simpson? Does you brood arrive like battery eggs on a conveyor belt? We're surrounded by some of the most glorious scenery in all the world but can it for one moment distract you from your snivelling dislike of a harmless dog?'

The class, as they were expected to, tittered at the dialogue but Simpson was determined. A transient population of all types of dogs had passed through his easygoing household, no one caring where they came from or where they went to and Simpson, thrice bitten, was trebly shy. If experience is a hard master its lessons are not quickly forgotten and

Simpson now had a very sound instinct about dogs. He placed no trust in the big yellow dog with the big yellow fangs that in his judgement was going to turn itself into a gauntlet to be run. Simpson tried again.

'Please, sir, when they bare their teeth like that and when the hair sticks up on their shoulders—'

'Silence! At home I have an Alsatian and if I feared him he would master me. The secret of handling dogs is courage, a quality I've yet to perceive in your make-up.' He paused for the class to giggle. 'Dogs can smell fear. They can also smell courage, and know by instinct the man who can master them. There's nothing to be afraid of. You'll all walk by on the verge and I'll stay on the road and reassure the dog we mean him no harm. Come on, in twos, jump to it.'

As his class made a two by two crocodile across the road from the caravan the teacher strode boldly up the centre of the road to prove his point. The children came along like a train shunting, those behind pushing those in front, and the van was not a popular place at all.

Nearly all dogs are possessive to some degree of masters and territories. The dog that lives in suburbia will look on the garden gate as its territorial limit, farm dogs are usually jealous of all the farmyard and outbuildings, but Juttal had no such permanent landmarks to look upon as his own. He lived where they happened to stay the night but that is not to say he did not define the area of the land belonging temporarily to him. His mobile hermit of a master craved the company of no man and on the rare occasions they made camp with other gipsies he always kept some distance between his old home and the modern trailers of his brothers. And in some inexplicable canine way Juttal had built an invisible but inviolable perimeter round the caravan, when it was parked for the night, at a distance of about twenty feet. In this case Juttal's home ground ended almost exactly in the dead centre of the drove-road—the reason for his warning off the tractor.

As the school party came closer, Juttal kept his eyes on the teacher who was walking just on the wrong side of the centre of the road. The nearer the teacher came the more Juttal's upper lip lifted and the drawn out growl changed to a snarl. The teacher was not short of courage and in normal circumstances he was not a fool; his blind spot was dogs, but this time, as Juttal's warning became more fearsome, he realised with neck-prickling suddenness that he had made a mistake. This dog was not going to be mollified by kind words and petting and the snarled warning was not bluff. This dog was deadly serious and the teacher should have used the situation to show his class that there can always be exceptions to rules. After his good-natured ridiculing of Simpson he could not bring himself to do that, so he compounded his mistake by foolhardily pressing on at a slower pace.

The crocodile was filing by him swiftly now, eager to get out of the danger zone where the dog had eyes only for the teacher, and with a concerted run they put twenty yards between themselves and the caravan, then stopped to watch with excited whispers.

The teacher had one yard to go and his

foot would cross the fatal, invisible ring and Juttal saw this as an attack. His head went lower, his hind quarters bunched, his mouth opened a little and his snarl was terrifying.

'Now then,' the teacher smiled softly, 'you're not frightened of me, are you lad?' He was inching forward with his right palm out, nearly on top of Juttal's boundary. 'You know I won't hurt you, I want to be friends. I—'

Juttal's lean body came off the ground with the speed of a cobra, the long narrow jaws slashed at the extended hand and the teacher fell over backwards and rolled in the white dust. He squirmed round to face the attack with blood dripping from two torn fingers, expecting to fight for his life but Juttal had retreated. The teacher was outside the camp boundary again, the dog on the inside and still threatening but no more. The snarl was reduced to a growl again and the teacher got an inkling of what he had done wrong. He walked quickly along the far verge to join the children.

The girls were all concern, the boys wanted a look at his injuries and he did not look directly at Simpson who would be smirking. Simpson, he told himself ruefully, was entitled to smirk. Belatedly he pointed out that Juttal was a perfect example of the exception to normal procedure they must be prepared to meet from time to time and that, although the dog was obviously doing no more than perform a duty he had been trained to, he was a danger loose on public land and the remedy was to report him to the police. They would do that as soon as possible and return to the coach waiting on the main road by another route. Furthermore, the outing would end before the planned time as he would need an injection against tetanus. He turned a deaf ear to whatever Simpson was whispering to his pals. He was not vindictive.

Juttal waited until the party was out of sight and slouched back under the caravan. He did not rest for long, his hunger pains had increased too much to ignore.

He went out into the open again and restlessly paced about, up and down the side of the road, occasionally watching the horse.

In the middle of the afternoon he went for a drink and returned to continue his pacing. He brought the horse back once, not understanding that the horse too needed water and when the rim of the sun touched the skyline Juttal could wait no longer. He had to have food. He set off for the escarpment.

In the dying twilight he scrambled down the first short slope on to a narrow plateau. He looked over the second lip and the light was good enough to see them hopping about on a gentler incline behind a clump of bushes thirty feet beneath him. The rabbits. Families of them.

First there was the obstacle of the steep drop to get around. Silent on the thick grass he ran to the north along the edge of the small cliff always, but only slightly, descending. As the ground below was always rising, soon it was only a leap of six feet to the level below. Juttal jumped, turning as he hit the ground with his saliva running

In the last light of the day he came to the rabbits' playground and paused behind one of the bushes. They were everywhere, popping behind and out from behind rocks and tree trunks and bushes, darting in and out of the burrows.

He did not hesitate more than a second, charging from his cover and landing in the middle of them a few feet from a large buck. They were quick as rabbits in danger are and burst outward, away from the intruder, vanishing into holes with the acceleration of fear. Juttal's buck started to spring away at the first sound of heavy paws hitting the ground behind him but he was making a standing start and Juttal was into his stride and the buck never had a chance. Its neck was cleanly broken by a twisting jerk of Juttal's head and Juttal did not wait about. He was on his way back to the caravan with the warm, sagging body still in the final spasm of twitching.

Juttal's diet was the same as Albert's, nearly all meat, and he could take it as it came, raw or cooked, but the raw meat had always been skinned or plucked for him and he set off automatically back to where he could have it prepared by the only person who would skin it for him.

Holding the buck possessively in his mouth he stood looking up at the closed caravan door, just discernable in the starlight, and whined for help. He stayed there a long time, holding his prize, his contracted stomach shrinking and shrinking until the numb ache became real sharp pain.

When the moon was high and his jaws aching with the weight of the buck he let it drop and regarded it a while with cocked head. The only barrier to the juicy meat was a layer of fur and he could wait no longer. He would remove the fur himself.

There on the centuries-old drove-road he put his forepaws on the rabbit's body, took a hind leg in his mouth and pulled, and took his first step backward in time. He was fending for himself without the aid of man.

Over thousands of years dogs have become so dependent on man that most of them—especially city bred dogs— would very likely starve in a countryside running wild with game. They would not connect the meals served to them with a running rabbit, a timid hen or a docile cow and if they did they would not know how to go about killing and getting at the flesh. Juttal was fortunate. He was already a trained and skilful hunter, a slaughterman, and his plight forced him into learning how to be a butcher. It was a matter of holding the buck firmly enough and tearing at the right place. The task demanded all the strength of his neck and shoulders and he had to swallow a lot of fur. But he was eating, satisfying the second priority of any animal.

There was not much of the buck left when Juttal's belly was at last full: the head, the offal and some ribs. A truly wild dog would have been jealous of the remains, remembering past hungers and poor hunting, and would have carefully buried the leavings. For Juttal enough was enough. He sighed, licked the last of the flesh taste from his lips and went under the caravan to sleep. He would not hunger again, he had all the wild cascading escarpment for his larder.

It was late when he was wakened. The plod of hooves thrumming through the ground first stirred him. It was only the horse. Cosily he was drifting off again when he was alerted by a human voice. A strange one.

'Anyone in?'

Juttal was a tawny missile when he left his bed. He shot out on to the verge and stopped at his private boundary. A strange man had the horse by the halter, a man too wise and discreet to go too close when he saw the big dog sleeping. He was a fat man with the slow North Riding accent and smile. He gave the horse a slap and sent it into Juttal's circle.

'Anyone in? Your 'oss wandered up to our farm.' He waited a few more moments and looked at Juttal's fangs. 'I'm bloody glad I didn't try to knock on the door.' He turned and went back the way he had come, stopping a hundred yards away to look at the camp thoughtfully. 'It's not like a gipsy to go off an' leave his animals. I'll 'ave to see about it.'

Juttal stayed at his post until it was clear the man would not come back. The morning dragged on the same as the day before. Juttal went for a drink and kept the horse close to home. He was snoozing out of the hot sun by the side of the caravan when the car engine came into earshot. He watched with cocked ears from where he lay. Cars are not people, they are impersonal machines, not like tractors where the driver is a visible threat, and he was ready to let the car go by unchallenged. Except the car did not go by, it pulled up close to the verge, on the wrong side of its legal limit according to Juttal's sense of what was proper. It was still only a car but now he stood up to watch it and was fired into action when the door opened and a blue-trousered leg came out. Juttal went for the leg which smartly disappeared and the door slammed inches from his nose. Now it was only a car again, his hackles smoothed and he stopped snarling.

Inside the car the policeman's mate laughed, 'Go on, Bill, it's only kiddin'.'

'Is it?' grunted Bill, picking up the microphone to contact his sergeant. 'We're at the scene of the complaint, sarge, and the schoolteacher was right, this dog'll have you as quick as look at

64

you.'

The sergeant's amusement came through as clear as his metallic voice, 'It's not only a complaint, Bernard Jackson reckons there's summat wrong, the gipsy's probably poorly or summat. Just knock on the door and find out, son, eh? Try talkin' to the dog through the window first, it'll be all right.'

'Right, sarge.' Bill wound down his window and looked out at Juttal who watched with curiosity. Bill had been brought up at Helmsley, a few miles away; he was a countryman and liked all animals. He said very gently, 'Now then, old lad, what's up—'

He had his hand on the knob and only just got the window up before Juttal was in the car with them.

'Christ, Johnny,' he breathed, 'I reckon that dog must have been ill-treated at some time to act like that.' He called up his sergeant again.

The sergeant heard him out and was deliberately condescending. 'I know how it is, lad, when you're not used to dogs. I remember when I was on the beat—bikes then, not cars—an' there was this dog—

I'll tell you that story over a pint sometime. Just now, you'd better hang on there a bit an' I'll see about sendin' somebody that knows how to handle dogs.'

Bill put down his microphone, 'Big-headed sod.'

Johnny laughed, 'He's mates with the RSPCA and Jim McConnachie, one of 'em'll be up soon. Relax.'

Juttal lay down in the shade now that the car was only a car again. And the car held so little interest for him that he fell asleep. He woke once at the click of a door handle but dropped off again at the second click when the door was quickly closed.

He was fully wakened when the second car drove up. This one stopped some distance away, the driver getting out and beckoning to the police car. The police car reversed to join him and the three men stood talking. The newcomer was tall, competent-looking, middle-aged with iron-grey hair. His face was coloured by many hot summers and hard winters. His smile held the same amusement as the sergeant's voice.

66

'Now then, what's the trouble?'

'We're supposed to have a look in the caravan but the dog won't let us near,' Johnny told him.

'Och, well now,' Jim McConnachie smiled slowly. 'Let's see what we can do.' from the back of his car he took a metal tube about six feet long with a rope noose at one end. The tail rope of the noose ran through the tube and after lassooing an animal the vet could hold it captive at a safe distance. He made the noose larger. 'If I can get this over his head we've nothing to worry about. Let's have a try.'

They started forward together but the vet told the policemen to hang back, 'I want him concentrating on me, it gives me a better chance.'

Steadily, talking gently all the time, Jim McConnachie walked up to Juttal and Juttal's hackles and upper lip rose proportionately as the gap between them closed, the low growl became the high snarl and the long powerful muscles bunched.

It is true that dogs can detect fear in a human; it is not true that every dog will bow the knee in the face of courage and lower its colours any more than every lion will waive its attack because it can hear the strains of Mendelssohn's Spring Song. Animals are as individual as man with all the traits of bravery and cowardice. There are frank animals and sneaks, fun lovers and sour faces. One thing Jim McConnachie's forty years of vetting had taught him was never to take any animal for granted and to assume the worst until he found out what kind of patient he was treating at first hand. He had also picked up a lot about animal psychology and possibly understood the simple canine mind as well as anyone, but never forgot it can be surprisingly capricious.

The first thing any handler must do is gain the dog's undivided attention and this was one time that often lengthy job was no task at all. Juttal's eyes were fixed on his with single-track malevolence.

Jim stopped just short of the length of the tube from Juttal, his instinct telling him he had gone as far as he would be allowed. He did not stop talking, a soothing flow that was meaningless babble to the dog and he kept running his left hand through his hair to hold Juttal's eyes upward as he pushed the noose along the ground with his right. Experienced as he was he did not relish the consequences of fluffing the only attempt he would get at trapping this fierce sentinel.

Jim did not let the stalemate last long. He knew the initiative was his, if the dog had been going to attack for the sake of it it would have had its teeth into him by then, but anything might happen to disturb the balance of the situation and those fangs were large and sharp—and willing.

When he pushed his hand through his hair for the third time he had the stiff sisal noose where he wanted it, directly under and a foot away from Juttal's head. With a flick of a wrist that had wrestled with more than one bull the noose dropped over Juttal's head, Jim's left hand simultaneously snatching at the tail rope to tighten the noose. Juttal's natural reaction was to pull away and the vet went with him, drawing in the last of the slack and gripping tail rope and tube with both hands.

When Juttal found he could not pull away he reversed his tactics, tried a counter attack, and got the same result. When he pulled the man came with him, when he charged the man retreated before him. Always the rope gripped his neck and the strong tube was a perfect barrier. When he had tried both moves twice Juttal panicked, snarling and snapping trying to leap in every direction, aware of nothing but his urge to be free. And none of it was the slightest use.

Throughout the exhibition of vicious anger Jim McConnachie kept up the flow of quiet, friendly chatter but he knew that when the dog stopped trying to break away, when it stood bristling and trembling, it was not because of any calming influence of his. The dog realised that for the moment it was helpless and would never escape while the noose held tight, but it was quick and strong and would instantly take advantage of any careless mistake. Jim even tightened his hold a little, 'All right, you can go have a look now, take your time, I can hold him.'

This statement was put to the test when the policemen went to the caravan. When they crossed the boundary, Juttal barked and snarled, when one of them climbed on the box-seat and knocked on the door, Juttal exploded. It was well Jim McConnachie was expecting something of the kind.

He was dragged five paces by Juttal's charge at the two men invading his property, literally digging in his heels and throwing back all his thirteen stones to halt the dog. Juttal strained on, the short grass giving his paws a good hold, Jim heaved back, thanking again whatever power had blessed him with a big strong body. A dog weighing six stones is, pound for pound, stronger than a man twice its weight and the vet was grateful the fact went no further than the comparison. As it was, because four points of contact with the ground give better traction than two, Juttal's pulling power almost exactly equalled the vet's. Like a Husky he strained into the noose, frantic to drive off the intruders, thrusting with every ounce of strength in

71

his superb muscles until the rope closed his windpipe. He coughed, pulled back, sucked in air, threw himself forward again.

'Steady on, there,' Jim gasped, 'you'll strangle yourself.' As if understanding, Juttal turned on him, quickly, leaping high again and again, with Jim playing him like a fish.

The policemen had entered the caravan which was unlocked and when they came out Bill went to the car. When Johnny followed him Juttal surprised the vet by the way he stopped fighting. The struggle had taken them across the road to the far verge and now that there were no strangers within the limits of the camp site the Lurcher stood as if reviewing his predicament.

'There now,' Jim praised him, 'that's better. No need to kill yourself.' He called to Johnny who was standing outside the car, 'Trouble?'

'The old man's dead. Two or three days it smells like. Phew.'

'What about this feller?'

Johnny shrugged. 'The dog? I don't know, Bill'll get onto the sergeant when

72

they've contacted the ambulance depot.'

'You'll have to do something about the dog, I can't stay much longer, I've four calls this afternoon and I'm late now.'

Johnny grinned. 'You can get off now. If you can leave the dog-catcher, I'll hold him till some arrangement's made.'

The vet showed the policeman how to hold the tube with the tail rope wrapped around one hand and instructed, 'No tighter than that or you'll be choking him. And don't take your eyes off him, he's quick off the mark and as strong as a horse.'

Carefully, they transferred Juttal into Johnny's custody with Juttal watching suspiciously. Jim rubbed the back of his left hand and flexed the fingers. If he starts acting up go with him all the time and he can't hurt himself. Just watch him when anyone goes up to the caravan. You'll drop the catcher off for me at the surgery?'

'We will, and thanks. I reckon a couple of coppers owe you a couple o' pints.'

'I'll keep you to that.' Jim McConnachie went on his way to deal with more amiable patients.

Bill came from the car with two lighted cigarettes and gave one to Johnny. 'The ambulance is on the way and the sarge is tryin' to get in touch with the RSPCA.' He blew smoke at Juttal, 'Looks quiet enough now. Must know he's been gaffered.'

Johnny held his cigarette in his mouth and took a fresh grip on the tube. 'Let's test him, walk over to the caravan.'

Casually Bill strolled away and started a rumble deep in Juttal's throat. The rumble became the growl and the growl the snarl and when Bill put a hand on the box-seat as though to climb up Juttal went berserk again, his steely thighs catapulting him straight up off the ground, the only way he could go. Feet astride and prepared as he was, Johnny nearly overbalanced with the first lunge, but he quickly got the knack of holding on and preventing Juttal as far as possible from injuring himself. When the frustrated dog turned on him he moved backward a few paces, spat out his cigarette and shouted, 'That'll do.'

Bill came off Juttal's territory shaking his head. 'Whatever else he is, he's bloody loyal to that old man.'

'Maybe so, but I won't be sorry when the RSPCA take him off our hands.'

Juttal panted, watched and waited.

They went through it all again when the ambulance arrived and Albert's body came out on the stretcher. Like something demented Juttal fought the noose, trying alternately to get at the trespassers or Johnny, leaping high, twisting and turning or attempting to haul Johnny bodily, the savage rage glaring from his maddened eyes. The ambulance bumped away and Juttal quietened again.

The call sign for their car crackled out and Bill ran across for instructions.

'That bloody sergeant's a sadist,' he said when he had switched off the transmitter. 'He says the RSPCA'll be a couple of hours and we can take the dog into the station and stop loafin' about up here, or else make it secure and get round the beat. What d'you reckon?'

'I reckon we're not goin' to try to get it in the car. We could tie it to the caravan.'

'Good idea, son. Go on, then.'

Johnny had been holding Juttal for more than half an hour, the fingers of his left hand white and numb. 'You're as big a sadist as the sergeant. You hold him a minute while I get the circulation back in my hand then we'll figure out how we can do it.'

'No stamina,' Bill grunted. 'Give us hold, then.'

Carefully they started the transfer. Bill took the end of the tube as Johnny slipped the turns of rope from his hand, at the same time trying to keep the noose snug around Juttal's neck. It happened as Bill was taking the rope and saying, 'Talk about Laurel and Hardy.' Juttal felt the tension of the noose ease and his reflexes did the rest. A sideways pull, a backward wriggle and he was free. Another instinctive action almost cost him that freedom when he stood still for the luxury of a thorough shake. The centre of the violent rippling shudder had not reached his rump when Bill made a quick cast with the noose. The noose tipped Juttal's nose and he reared away, ran inside his boundary and turned to face them.

'You've done it now,' said Johnny smugly.

'Get knotted, it was your fault but I'll catch him again.' The vet had demonstrated how easy it was and Bill copied him—or tried to. Ten minutes, half a dozen unsuccessful tries and a bite on the wrist later he withdrew and gave the lasso to Johnny. 'You let him go, you get him back.' He went to the car for the first aid box.

Juttal's teeth marks were deep front and back of the wrist but they had missed the arteries and the blood welled slowly. Johnny covered the wounds with Elastoplast, 'First thing for you is an anti-tetanus jab and I don't think there's any need to catch the dog again. He'll stay here guarding the caravan, that's his job, till the RSPCA get here.'

'You're right, an' while I'm queueing at the hospital you can go in and tell the sergeant all about it. I think I'd sooner be bitten again than face him.'

When the car had gone Juttal brought the horse back and settled down for a rest. It was a busy life without Albert.

# CHAPTER 3

Nothing else happened that day except that the horse disappeared. Juttal lazed about keeping an eye on things until mid-afternoon when he got thirsty and went for a drink. It was three-quarters of a mile to his rivulet, a round trip of about fifteen minutes if he had not been distracted, but he had seen and stalked a pheasant. The pheasant had seen him and beaten him into the air, then he had had fun chasing the squirrels aloft. He had never caught a squirrel but there was a special excitement about trying to catch the furry little creatures that could run as fast vertically as he could laterally, or so it seemed.

Then he had almost walked on to a cat, a scarred old tom that was stalking a sparrow, and of course Juttal had no choice but to prove canine superiority over the antedeluvian foe. The cat was angry that Juttal had cost him a meal, but not enough to stand and fight. The cat too took to the trees, balancing easily on a branch ten feet out of Juttal's reach, glaring down with soulless green eyes, hissing in return to Juttal's barking. At the stream there was more fun with the frogs but he did not catch a frog, either.

He lapped a long time at the sweet tinkling water and returned to the camp at what was for him a sedate stroll. When he got there the horse was gone. He searched a long way up and down the road in both directions but there was neither sight nor scent of the old fellow.

He did another period of guard duty, dozing or prowling until the sun was low and he was getting hungry. He did not go hunting just then, they—Albert and he—waited until the twilight was dropping and the rabbits leaving the burrows, so Juttal lay waiting for the light to start fading. Already Albert was coming less into his thoughts as he thought about feeding himself. The rabbits were there again when he looked over the cliff, playing, feeding or sitting by the mouths of the burrow staring at nothing. He went by the same route down to the rabbits' plateau, leaping amongst them and taking a young doe. He took it home to the caravan but set about eating it at once. There was an extra satisfaction somehow in getting through the fur to the warm flesh unaided. Replete once more he settled down for the night in his normal place.

Juttal had no grumbles, no complaints, he was self-sufficient. His way of life with Albert had taught him if not actually to hate strangers at least to regard them with suspicion, and unlike most of his kind he did not need company, of man or dog. It was enough for him to go and come as he liked, chase other animals or birds when he wanted and help himself to a rabbit each evening.

'Alan!'

Alan finished totting up the figures, found his first total to be correct and Archie bawled again, 'Alan!'

Alan put the ledger away in the drawer of the kitchen table and went out into the yard. The bright morning did not reflect the situation at Lane End farm. For the moment they were not slipping back any more, but they were not progressing, either. He crossed the yard to the barn where Archie was waiting sitting on the tractor's front wheel.

'No good, she won't start.' he grumbled. 'U' don't have this trouble with 'osses.'

Alan sighed, tired of Archie promoting a return to draught-horses. He took a piece of stiff wire from a nail in the wall and started to tie a ball of rag to one end, 'Get the air filter off.'

'It's off.'

'Ready, then.'

Alan dipped the rag into a bucket of paraffin, set it burning with his lighter and held the blaze to the air intake. Archie cranked the starting handle, grumbling again, 'Right bloody game this is.' He was grinning when he said it. Alan could only agree with him. The starter motor was worn out and the engine needed a rebore. Because of the lost compression it was now routine procedure to start up by giving the engine hot air to breathe. Half a dozen times

Archie swung the handle before the big diesel roared and belched black smoke out into the yard, putting a curious chicken to flight. Alan held up a hand, left Archie to it and went back to the house to write to the Young Farmers' Association turning down their request for him to give an after-dinner talk on the differences in American and British farming. He just did not feel like it.

Alice was out working in the vegetable garden, he shouted through the open window that he would not be back until dinner time and drove slowly up the bumpy lane to the road.

He went eastward for a mile, turning off into a lane even worse than the farm road, climbing the side of a hill. The track ended a mile and a half from the road at the gate of Mannie Fairbrother's garden. Brenda Fairbrother's pet, a rubber ball of a Jack Russell, barked the alarm and came bouncing out to meet Alan. The tiny dog escorted him to the cottage, jumping to waist height all the way and yapping its welcome.

'Cup o' tea?' Brenda asked as he entered the low room.

'Might as well, Mannie moans if I tap him for one out of his flask.'

'You lot are worse than women for tea.'

In other days and other places she, along with her husband, would have made a good pioneer. A robust five feet six with enviable health and strength she was carrying her first baby with the aplomb of a seasoned child bearer. The daughter of a smallholder in the village of Sutton-Under-Whitestone-Cliff at the bottom of the escarpment, she was acquainted with nature's mysteries. As a toddler she had been present at the birth of lambs, pigs, cows, and dogs and expected her delivery to be just as natural and easy.

With his tea she gave him a large wedge of cheese and onion pie and, as he always did, he complimented her on the pastry.

'Fire oven, love,' Brenda laughed, 'Them electric an' gas cookers are no good, I wouldn't have one given.'

He stayed chatting for half an hour and started the climb up to the higher pasture, to where Mannie was moving the flock.

He did not follow the track angling up the hillside but he went by the shortest route to the spine of the ridge, sitting down at the top to get his breath back and smoke a cigarette.

Seven miles to the south-west he could see as a tiny speck the gliding club buildings and the Piper Cub climbing away with a glider in tow. The aeroplane was about four miles away; someone wanted plenty of height for a long spell upstairs. Alan wished it was him.

His own farm was less than a mile away as the crow flies, looking very neat and tidy at the distance. A very neat and tidy white elephant, he thought. The thought spoiled the panorama for him. He got up and walked along the ridge; Mannie would be over the next dip. He was. Sitting on a rock whistling the dogs into urging the flock along the hillside where he would let them start grazing methodically. Alan sat with him and for all his experience still wondered at the way these shepherds work in such harmony with their unkempt dogs. When Mannie had the sheep where he wanted them Alan observed, 'The young 'un seems to be comin' on all right.'

'I reckon he'll do,' Mannie nodded, taking a quart-sized flask from an old haversack. 'Fancy a cup?'

'No, ta, I found a lonely bird back there who fed and watered me. Mugs these fellers that go out leaving their women all day.'

'As long as you didn't eat all the pie.' They sat quiet a while watching the flock beginning to graze its way down the hill, part of the stock on which Alan was relying to help him out of trouble. He shaded his eyes.

'How's that sickly ewe coming on?'

'Aw, she'll be okay, Jim's coming to have another look at her in the mornin' but he sez there's nowt to worry about now.' Mannie chuckled. 'Yesterday afternoon he was tellin' me about a do he had with a dog. That old gipsy what camps down on the drove-road pegged out an' this Lurcher wouldn't let anyone near. I saw it down on the Bottoms a couple o' days ago but it took off when I shouted.'

'After rabbits, I suppose. What

happened?'

'Jim got the dog on a rope an' handed it over to the Highway Patrol an' it got away from them. Seems the sergeant went blue and gave 'em a right bollockin', so young Johnny's missus was tellin' Brenda on the telephone.'

'So everything's all right then up here? Anything you want?'

'Not that I can think of off-hand. Arey' off for a pint tonight?'

'I expect so, about half eight.'

'I'll be there, don't forget your darts, we'll take a few pints off the Highway Patrol if they're off duty.'

'Right, see you.' Alan returned to the car by the shelving track, refused another snack and drove east when he got to the road.

He drove steadily along the narrow roads, picking up the A170 at Helmsley and turning into a service garage two miles from the small town. The girl sitting reading in the kiosk by the pumps waved as he went to the house. He entered without knocking.

'Joan!'

'Won't be a minute,' she shouted from

upstairs.

Alan went into the living-room to stand at the window and watch the Land-Rover tow a battered Cortina across the forecourt into the garage.

Joan Atkins, widowed five years, had the common sense to learn about the business from her husband and the intelligence to run it profitably with the help of her eighteen-year-old daughter. The three mechanics were mostly occupied with repairing farming machinery and in summer when the tourists and holiday makers came out the petrol sales soared encouragingly. Like Alan, Joan was in her forties and was very much an older version of Brenda Fairbrother; unshakable, a born optimist who believed adamantly in silver linings.

When she came down Alan grinned and wolf-whistled. She was wearing jodhpurs and a very tight green sweater.

'Less of that,' she grinned, 'it's shrunk in the wash. I didn't expect to see you today.'

'I got fed up, fancied a few hours off.'

'Good, you can have the gelding, a

hard gallop'll knock the miseries out of you.'

Joan was a fairly good horsewoman, a regular entrant in the local shows who got her share of the prizes and ran a non-profit-making small riding school behind the garage. The stables were all that remained of the farm which had originally stood on the site: six stalls housing Joan's mare, her daughter's gelding and four assorted ponies.

They went out the back way, trotting in single file along the narrow lane for a mile to the edge of the moorland, then going into a canter until Joan shouted, 'Race you!'

The upward gradient was slight, the dry stone walls low, the horses full of running and enthusiasm for the impromptu steeplechase. They raced on for a mile, easily clearing the walls with Joan increasing her lead and looking back to shout, 'Aren't you coming?' He answered with a cowboy yell. She had beaten him, she said, by a distance and was sitting on a wall getting out a cigarette when he dismounted. Alan did not ride very often. Breathing heavily he hitched up on to the wall, took the cigarette packet from her hand and lit up for both of them.

'Old Man River,' she smiled.

'It's all right for you ladies of leisure, I don't get the practice.'

'You should do this more often instead of loafing about sitting in that death trap you fly. That's not exercise.'

He took her hand, held it on his knee, 'Let's not start that again.'

Always cheerful, Joan was more light-hearted than usual with Alan. Knowing his problems and his strong sense of independence, the last thing he needed was sympathy. She felt it, naturally but kept it to herself.

'Well, how's it coming along?'

'Could be worse. I reckon I'm holding my own now, a decent summer and I should be pulling round.'

'And if you do have a good year?'

Alan drew on his cigarette, eyes fixed on the hazy distance to the south. She squeezed his hand hard. 'What about us?'

'We've been through it all before, I'll have to get the farm on its feet first—'

'And how long's that going to take? Five years if you're lucky but more like ten. I'm over forty *now*, Alan, it's not fair to ask me to go on waiting. If the worst happens and the farm fails we'll have the garage and it's a good living and—'

'And it's yours and Barbara's. You can't expect me to just move in like some ponce. And the farm's not going to fail, I'm going to make it crack, we've got everything lined up now, you'll see.'

Joan dropped from the wall, not exactly angry but stirred to a fighting mood to battle for what she wanted. 'And I still say you're not being fair to me. Barbara thinks the world of you, she wouldn't mind if the worst should happen...and just say it did, what then? I suppose I can take it we'll never get married?' This was the closest they had come to having a stand-up row in their three years together and it was the first time she had raised the question of what would happen if the farm did go to the wall. She was well within her rights, she deserved a concrete answer. He looked at her then and all he saw in her face was concern.

'All right, love,' he said quietly, 'I want one more year and then rain or shine we'll get married if you still want to.'

Juttal shook himself, stretched his left hind leg and then his right. He yawned gapingly and then made a circuit of the camp. The dew was heavy that morning, a million reflections making a glistening track to the low sun. Juttal scythed his head, tongue lapping in the large drops clinging to the grass.

He was restless that morning, uneasy at camping in one place too long. By now they should have been far to the south on the lower leg of their perpetual journey which paused annually in the field with many other caravans and dogs and horses. Many, many horses and noisy men who galloped the horses up and down, shouting, bartering, exchanging. Juttal had no particular love for the big fair or for any other loud overpopulated place but it was a regular landmark and must be visited. However, his home was the caravan and the caravan did not move and he would stay with it.

The horse was not here where it should be and it must be found, brought back to where it belonged. He scanned in all directions without sighting it and started out randomly to the south. One direction was as good as another.

There was a farm near the junction, where another road led off to the east, but he ignored the farm and the turn off and went on to where the main road wound down the steep face of Sutton Bank to the west with gradients as steep as one in four. Going eastward the road led to the coast twenty-four miles away but Juttal had never been to the sea.

The North Yorkshire Moors National Parks Committee have thoughtfully provided a broad clear space close to the top of Sutton Bank for visitors to leave their cars while they go to admire the view from the very lip of the escarpment. There were several vehicles parked there when Juttal loped across it.

Some of the families were having picnic meals and belonging to one motorised caravan were two dogs, nondescript mongrels who were hanging about hopefully for scraps. They were both medium-sized, well-nourished and thoroughly spoiled animals who ignored everything but their own whims. A young boy threw a piece of meat in a high curve. One of the dogs leapt, twisting athletically to catch it in mid air, and as he hit the ground he saw Juttal.

The mongrel gulped down the titbit, braced his forelegs and barked aggressively. This drew the attention of his running mate who joined in to make it a double challenge. Juttal gave them one look and went about his business of searching for the horse. He had reached the centre of the car park when he heard the dogs coming. He also heard the angry shouting of the dogs' owner and understandably thought it was directed at him, who had often been yelled at and chased away from farm gates he had no intention of entering. He would have ignored the shouts, shouts do not hurt, but he could not ignore the dogs who were flying across to attack him.

He did not know that these city dogs had much more bark than bite, that they would have stopped a couple of yards

93

from him quite content with a barking match. They did not know what kind of no-nonsense opponent they had picked.

With the bewildering speed of his father he jack-knifed sideways and drove in low at the nearest mongrel. His teeth went into the side of the neck, luckily seizing on loose skin and hair; he heaved up, throwing the dog on its back, spun and jumped at the second one. This one had never bitten anything in anger, raucous barking was the closest it ever came to violence, and if its master had trained it to be obedient, it would not have been so badly mauled. Juttal tore its shoulder and chest before the first mongrel recovered and came to assist and the three of them rolled in a locked knot.

Over the barking of the mongrels and Juttal's high pitched snarls human voices raised in alarm yelled contradictory orders for them to stop. So fierce was the fight no one risked trying to separate the dogs and it ended only when both mongrels fled yelping. Juttal stood a few seconds as if undecided whether to pursue and re-engage and a young boy took advantange by throwing a stone at him. The stone missed and had no bearing on Juttal's decision to let well enough alone. He had a shake, turned about and went on his way.

'Some people aren't fit to have dogs,' moaned the owner of the injured and badly shaken mongrels.

In the time it took for Juttal to cross the car park and turn east along the road he had forgotten the incident, the nips on his shoulder and rump were nothing. The road was fairly straight and he could see a long way into the distance. The horse was not in sight. And when a pheasant flew up out of the thick wood on his right he forgot the horse, simply going on his way to see what he could see. He had gone on for perhaps a mile when a car overtook him, slowing and parking a hundred yards ahead. When the two men got out he saw that they were the same pair he had escaped from the day before. One of them tilted his cap back.

'It's him all right. There's no other Lurchers round here and he's no collar on.'

Juttal slowed as he got nearer,

watching them in that oblique canine way and moving over to the far verge.

'Good dog.' Johnny crooned, squatting on his heels and holding out a friendly hand. 'Come on, then, that's a good lad.'

'And what,' Bill asked sarcastically, 'do you reckon you'll do if he comes?' Johnny was not given the chance to show his intentions. With a prolonged low growl that sounded like distant thunder Juttal trotted by, well wide of them.

'I don't know what I'd've done, but one thing's certain, that dog wants catchin' for his own good as much as anything else.'

'Aye, but I'm tryin' with me bare hands! It's a job for the RSPCA.'

Johnny got behind the wheel, 'Come on, let's see where he goes.'

With the danger behind him Juttal trotted nonchalantly on. He came to a cart track leading off to the left in the direction of the hills and that seemed as good a direction as any to explore. He made a large circle, skirting the foothills and passing five flocks of sheep. Three of the flocks were penned in closed fields and were unattended but the other two were on the open hillside and there were men and dogs with them. He gave them a wide, respectful margin.

His sharp trot covered many miles. He rejoined the drove-road far to the north of the campsite and made his way home in the late afternoon, but when he got there there was no home. The caravan had gone, there was only the cold dead fireplace with its black ashes. The disappearance of the horse had not bothered him too much but this was a disaster. He looked all around him as if expecting the caravan to pop out from behind a bush. Then he lay down on the slightly lighter patch of grass where the caravan had stood.

In his simple thought process he was at a loss. Roamers he and Albert were, always just arriving or just leaving somewhere, following the great circle up through the land of the lakes, the big sweep through the hills to the east and down again over the wide moors to the country that was heavily farmed and into the area of the towns and cities to where the fair was held.

The only place of permanence was the home on wheels and now that was gone. Albert, the horse, the caravan. Juttal had no anchor. He did not, could not reason, his actions hinged on instinctive reflex. The pattern of his life, as with all dogs, was dictated by habit, but he could not carry out what were traditions for him with the one, solid, central point of focus taken away. He was at that moment a puppet without strings reduced to considering only the most basic of his needs, hunger and thirst. As it was too early to eat, he slept.

He did not sleep long. His ears twitched at the approaching drone of an engine and he was instantly awake, head up. It was a small van, parking on Juttal's side of the road and when the driver wound down the window he had a friendly, plump face, a deep pleasant voice.

'Now then, old lad.' The man did not get out at once, but he sat quietly smoking a pipe as he inspected Juttal face to face without the insulation of the glass which would have made the meeting impersonal.

'They tell me you're a bit of a sod... you're not though, are you? Just ready to defend your own, eh, and you wouldn't be much of a dog if you didn't do that. That's the trouble with amateurs, they get hold of the wrong end of the stick. I think me'n you'll get along champion.'

Juttal saw nothing threatening in the quiet man. He was alert, ready for anything, but while the man kept his place he could stay there as long as he liked. For many long minutes they held their positions, the dog lying down but ready for anything, the man in the van talking, talking, feeling for the best way to take the dog.

Graham Maxwell had been with the RSPCA for most of his working life. His job was not work to him and if he had been a rich man he would have been happy to spend his time helping animals free of charge. He had a rare affinity with animals that came from his love of all living creatures from a daisy to a whale. He knew what was most likely to happen to Juttal when he caught him. No one would want an abandoned gipsy dog especially as he was getting on in

99

years—eight, seven at least and full of what most folk would call bad habits, and as he would be unclaimed there was but one alternative...there were too many unwanted dogs in the world already. But that would be kinder than letting him run wild and turn into a real menace. It was often a question of what was the kindest of limited alternatives.

Graham Maxwell put his hand through the window to knock out his cold pipe on the door handle. The innocent action brought Juttal's head up a little more and deep in his throat the rumbling started.

'Ha-ha. It looks to me as though you're still taking this as your own property. You might be and we'd better assume you are for my sake if all the police said about you's true. Mind you, I'll bet they were exaggerating a bit for sympathy.' He started his motor, reversed fifty yards and got out with a long leather lead, a chain choke collar and a paper bag. With the lead dangling and the bag held out prominently he began to walk back.

'How do you like a nice bit of raw liver, then? You'll be used to raw meat, not like our Whisky, he won't look at anything that's not cooked. That's the wife for you, treats him like a customer at the Ritz. Women, old lad, you're lucky, you don't have to deal with 'em...' He prattled on about nothing and everything, hoping his normal way of handling stray dogs would work. When he had ten yards to go he knew it would not. This big yellowish gipsy dog was on his feet, growling and showing his teeth and coming to meet him. Graham stopped with Juttal two yards from him. As long as Graham stayed still he was treated to the preliminary warning of the rumble, when he took a slow step forward he was given the imperative snarl. Graham took a chance. He retreated the single stride he had stolen and sat on the grass with the lead across his knees and started talking. Had Juttal understood he would have learned all about Graham's family and pets and the detached house on the outskirts of Thirsk; the timid Alsatian, ejected from some heartless person's car which he had had to chase all round the streets of the market town. That one, he assured

101

Juttal, had a happy ending. Graham's next-door-neighbour had taken the Alsation which was now thriving and basking in the love of a kind family. Maybe, he said without any conviction, Juttal's tale would end as happily. His friendly chatter had not the slightest effect on Juttal, whose contribution to the dialogue was an unpunctuated, rolling growl.

Graham took a small piece of liver from the bag and tossed it at Juttal's feet. Juttal stopped growling long enough to swallow it.

'Oh, you are a hard nut, aren't you.'

He threw another piece and got the same response. The third small lump he dropped a couple of feet in front of the dog and Juttal reached it by stretching his neck. The fourth landed nearer to Graham and Juttal gave him a further clue of what he was up against with the speed he darted out for the meat and back again. The next piece Graham put practically at his own feet and sat back, propping himself with his hands on the ground behind his back. With his eyes switching from the meat to the man

Juttal flashed out and in. Graham sighed. The liver was gone and now he had nothing to offer as a bribe. He sat up with crossed legs holding the lead up for Juttal to see, 'I shouldn't think you've ever worn one of these. They don't hurt but to tell the truth I don't fancy trying to get it on you. Don't go away.' He edged back another couple of yards before getting up and going to the van. He tossed the lead in through the open window and went round to open the back doors. Leaving them open he returned carrying something Juttal had seen before, a piece of equipment consisting of a rope and a tube.

The episode with the vet and policemen were still very fresh in Juttal's memory and he knew he had reason to be very wary of the instrument the man was carrying. It had not been a physically painful experience except when he had fought to drag away and nearly choked himself but it was captivity, not pain, that he feared. His neck had never known the feel of a collar, he had never even seen a kennel or a compound and he did not know there was any other way of life but his own. But his short taste of being under forcible control had been plenty for him. It would take the wiliest and quickest of men to get him into that position again. When the vet had so easily snared him he had been unprepared, taken completely by surprise when the noose jumped around his neck while he watched the man instead of the trap. Now he watched both with shuttling eyes.

Graham's system was different from Jim McConnachie's. Where Jim preferred insidious craft, Graham was all above board, making a game of it. Or trying to. He held the noose high for Juttal to see, waving it about in the hope that Albert had played with his dog. Albert had never done any such thing and Juttal only knew his own games of chasing squirrels and anything else that moved.

'There, boy, fetch it,' Graham laughed, flicking the noose to the ground on his right. Juttal snarled at the rope. Graham flicked it to his left and Juttal backed quickly as the arc it travelled brought it closer to him. If Graham was not having any success in enticing Juttal close enough to catch him, he *was* doing something no one else had. He was inside Juttal's imposed boundary with Juttal backing away in front of him.

'Come on, boy,' he shouted jovially, 'catch it, catch it!'

The noose swung high and hit the grass with a thump, back again high over Juttal's head with Juttal's eyes fixed on it whenever it moved. When the rope lay still he turned his snarl on Graham.

Graham stood letting the rope rest, wagging a finger at the dog. 'This is getting us nowhere and I want my tea. Let's see if the speed of my hand can deceive your eye.' He put out his left hand and flung it out to his left away from the noose and as he had expected Juttal's eyes went with it. Simultaneously he swung the rope up in his first serious attempt at getting it over the unwilling head. He failed again. Juttal was warned by the first fractional movement of the hand holding the tube and when the rope fell where his head should have been he was two yards away.

Graham tried again several times, only

for the dog to show how quickly he reacted to possible danger and in the end he gave up.

'What are we going to do with you? You're like a bloody eel and I'm going to want some help, that's obvious. It looks as though I'm going to have to get a net or something. But take it from me, I'll catch you. I've never been beaten yet and I'm not going to be. I shouldn't think you'll go far and I'll be back tomorrow.'

When he threw the hated noose into the back of the van, turned the van around and drove off, Juttal relaxed and realised he was thirsty and getting hungry. He trotted away to the escarpment.

He had not been gone long when the young boy came in from the fields on his tractor. He saw from a distance that the caravan had been taken away but would not have admitted to the relief he felt. Whenever there were gipsies in the district he was uneasy although none of them had ever offered to harm him. Deep-seated prejudices passed down the generations are hard to ignore. He stopped the tractor, jumped down and replaced the stones from Albert's hearth back on the dry wall from where they came. All that was left of the camp site was the patch of burned grass.

That evening Juttal did not take his kill home. He was used to sleeping under the caravan and now he would have to find something else to sleep under. Carrying his fair-sized buck he went on down the tricky slopes to the very bottom, along past the lake and up to the small cave that had carried the fox scent. He ate his meal outside in the flooding moonlight with the wispy clouds starting to race in the rising wind, the wind which rattled through the trees and ruffled his coat as he ate the last few mouthfuls. He licked every vestige of flavour from his chops, crouched and wriggled into the cave. Here it was dry, sheltered and with his robust health he was comfortably warm.

He had taken another step nearer to the primeval. He had made his home in a hole in the ground.

# CHAPTER 4

The change of weather was quick and unexpected, making fun of the television forecasters. The wind pushed heavy rain clouds in from the North Sea and from the plain the top of the escarpment was lost in the grey battering downpour. The opaque sheets billowed down with a drumming hiss which made the face of the escarpment a jigsaw of small torrents. Juttal lay in his hole watching it.

There was no point in getting wet for nothing. All living creatures would be sheltering in nests and dens just as Juttal was, staring dumbly. He did not see the lightning and the loud thunder crack startled him. He did not like the noise of thunder and nothing now would get him out of his hole until the rain stopped. Years before on such a loud crashing night when he had lain trembling under the caravan he saw a bolt strike a great tree quite close to the caravan. The sizzling blue light split the tree down the middle and it was lucky for Albert that the riven branches fell away from the caravan. All that mad roaring night Juttal had huddled behind a wheel, whimpering and whining in his fear of the unknown, the mighty forces he could not understand or fight.

Thunder and lightning were the only two things he was afraid of. He would always be wary of a looped rope but because of a lesson learned, not fear.

All that night and into the forenoon the storm kept him, nervously edgy, curled up in the hole, wincing at every celestial bang, blinking at the brilliant blue streaks. But as all things do, it ended. The thunder moved away to the west, the rain started to ease and the birds began to chirp and trill. When the sun made its first break through to the dripping, trickling world Juttal came out to shake and start living again. For a change he went west into the plain away from the escarpment and when he came to the road the heat of the sun was dispersing the water and there were tendrils of steam all along the tarmac.

Jim McConnachie rebandaged the paw of the last patient and the cat's lady owner put it in the basket and closed the lid. Jim gave her a small bottle of pills. 'Three times a day and the infection should clear up all right. Bring her back on Monday.'

Jim enjoyed every part of his job but the small animal side was his hobby horse. What was more he was at the time of life when dealing out cures from a warm surgery was much more attractive than squirming on the dirt floor of some icy barn up to the shoulders inside a cow.

'Shall I pour the tea, Jim?' his wife called from the kitchen.

'Yes, I won't be a minute.' He took off the long white smock and dropped it in the linen basket on his way to the kitchen. 'The sun's out at last. I might not get soaked after all.'

'Neither will I doing the shopping. How many calls have you?'

'Four unless anyone else rings in.' He took his tea to the window which looked from the side of the house along the road. 'Aye, I think it's going to get out all right.'

They were lucky, Jim and Paula McConnachie, and they knew it. More than man and wife, they were real good friends with the same love of the quiet country life that did not always turn out to be as quiet as expected. Such as the tiny mongrel pup they had adopted, an appealing scrap of life that had grown into a playful monster, a massive, benign animal that Jim thought might be half donkey. The gentle giant, Rufus, had latched on to and allowed himself to be ruled by Fred the old Boxer whose pugnacious face was an indelible lie. If anything—if possible—Fred was even softer and more affectionate than Rufus.

'They're a right pair,' Jim had once sighed, 'if we ever get burglars *we'll* have to protect the dogs.'

Fred ambled into the room with Rufus on his tail. When Paula had patted them both they went for Jim's contribution and lay at his feet. Rufus lay *on* his feet, looking up with a tongue-lolling grin. Paula laughed.

'It must be time to go. It beats me how they can tell.'

'Aye, they might be dumb but they're not daft.' He looked down at the expectant dogs, 'The pair of you can just wait till I've finished my elevenses.'

He never went anywhere without them. On his daily rounds, if he took Paula out for a meal, shopping expeditions or even formal dinner occasions, they were there on the back seat of the car, Fred seeming to scowl from one window and Rufus grinning from the other.

Jim put down his cup and had another look at the sky, 'Yes, I think I can—' He stopped and leaned across the draining board, peering up the road. 'Keep the dogs in,' he said quickly, striding over them and running from the room.

Paula tried to ask, 'What' but he was gone, hurrying up the corridor to the front door. The dogs automatically started to follow him, but she beat them to the door and shut them in the room. The car was parked in the drive at the front of the house, Jim stopped to get the dog-catcher and then went to stand just inside the gate, looking up the road over the hedge. When he heard Paula come out he held up a hand to stay her and she craned from the top step to see what he was up to. Coming from the east was a dog, a large spare dog that could only be the stray he had told her about. Jim made the noose bigger. Juttal was coming at a sharp trot, occupied with watching the hedge bottom for anything of note, one good cast of the noose as he passed and that would be one potential danger to the livestock removed. With five yards to capture to go Juttal stopped, cocked his head and faintly from the back of the house Jim heard the hullaballoo of Fred and Rufus complaining. What was faint to Jim was perfectly plain to Juttal but as he could not see who was making the din he turned to go on his way, but he did see the shape of the man through the privets. His natural distrust of all men but Albert saved him. He moved further out into the road, keeping an eye on the gateway and easily dodged the cast which was made more in desperation than conviction.

'Blast it!' Jim snapped as he threw the rope back in the car and hurried into the house, 'and blast those bloody dogs, can they no keep quiet one minute.'

Paula followed him. 'You can hardly blame the dogs and it's not really your job to round strays up.'

His quick flashes of irritation never lasted long and as he dialled a number he said quietly, 'It's everybody's job in a place like this swarming with lambs... Jim McConnachie here, Freda, is Graham in?...Good, yes please...Graham, that Lurcher's coming your way, I just missed getting him. If you come from your side I'll drive behind him till I see you, then we'll have him between us...yes...right, I'm on my way.' He snatched an old tweed jacket from the umbrella stand. 'I shouldn't be long.' When he slammed the car door and reversed into the road he did not hear the racket his own dogs created.

Juttal passed quickly through the village, sticking to the easy going on the roadside verge. Every now and then a vehicle swept by noisy and stinking, and behind him was a purr of a slowly-driven car that did not pass him. He was aware of it but

114

it offered no threat and when that engine noise stopped he forgot it. Up ahead on the other side of the road another vehicle had stopped and the driver was getting out, a driver Juttal knew, the plump man who had tried to put one of the gripping ropes around his neck. Juttal slowed his pace when the man came over to his side of the road and when he saw what the man was carrying he stopped. The man was coming at him with the same soft chatter, smiling, but with the noose out in front of him and Juttal backed away from it. Had a car passed at that moment he would have been caught, the engine roar and wind-rush would have covered the padding of carefully-placed feet and as it was his glance behind was only just in time. Another noose was swishing down at him, he twisted to his right, the rope catching his shoulder, ran across the road and jumped the hedge into the field to race away from the men and their cars and ropes. He veered right to the east to get back to the escarpment where it was safe.

'Well,' Graham shook his head, 'I think we're going to have something on catching that dog. It'd be easy if he was used to people. As it is...'

Jim nodded, 'Let's hope we can do it before he does any damage.'

'I've a feeling he won't, he's living on rabbits and there's plenty about and he hasn't offered to hurt anyone he didn't see as a threat. He's moved away from his old camp site, I'll have to try to find out where he's sleeping.'

At three miles the escarpment was a solid grey-green cliff stretching away to the north, the tumbling drops and plateaux masked by the distance and pale sunlight.

'You've a job on your hands finding him in that lot,' Jim observed.

'Oh, we'll do it. Everyone up there's keeping an eye out for him.'

'There'll be a few keeping an eye out for me this morning, I'm late. See you later, Graham.'

'Take care.'


When the alarm clock rang the strident clangour was a physical jolting in Mannie Fairbrother's head. He moaned pitifully. Brenda's bare arm smaked

116

from under the quilt to find the clock, she pressed the 'stop' button and Mannie, lying close up to her side, moaned again, 'Ta, love.'

She flung the quilt from his face, 'Up, get up, idle whack. It's nearly six.'

Like her, Mannie was one of those people who are instantly awake, who come from deep sleep to full alert without having to grope through a slothful fog. But last evening he, with Alan, had won eleven consecutive games of darts and had consequently drunk eleven pints of Old Peculiar, a dark heady draught beer that is not to be taken lightly or in too large doses. Now he was suffering and Brenda would see he paid in full.

The curtains of their cottage were never drawn and the pale golden light of the still morning was a hot weight on his eyelids. When he tried to cover his face again she kicked the quilt to the floor, singing loudly, 'Ohhh, it's nice to get up in the mornin' but it's nicer to stay in be-e-ed'

Mannie turned his back to the window, 'Don't, love,' he whispered.

'All right,' she bawled, bouncing from

the bed, 'what do you want me to give you next?... I know. TEN GREEN BOTTLES, HANGIN' ON THE WALL, TEN GREEN BOT—'

A pillow in the face shut her up but only momentarily. Dressing slowly she conducted a loud conversation with herself, listing the penalties to be suffered by those who overindulge. And Mannie did the only thing that would stop her, he got up, running naked through to the kitchen to let the Jack Russell out into the yard and put on the kettle. As the small dog dashed out the working dogs who slept in kennels ran in to say good morning. He gave each head a cursory pat, 'Right, outside again, I'll have to have time to come round this mornin'.'

Closing the door on them he went to the old brownstone sink to slosh his head and body with cold water. Gasping and streaming, he ran back to the bedroom and flicked at Brenda's bare back. She shrieked, snatched up a blouse and fled.

Vulnerable though Mannie was to the effects of alcohol, he had the resilience of youth, and when the scent of frying bacon drifted in to him he was ready to eat.

Mannie ate massively at breakfast to set himself up for the day, Brenda munched at a sandwich as she filled his flask and wrapped him a wedge of Wensleydale cheese.

'What d'you reckon to Alan?' she quizzed.

He pronged at the mushrooms. 'How d'you mean?'

'We-ell, he doesn't seem the same as he used to when he first set you on.'

Mannie swallowed and shrugged, 'He's a right to be fed up with the luck he's had, but that's farmin' an' he knows it. He'll pull round when things start to buck up. He's done well with Lane End after his old man nearly ran it into the floor.'

She put the flask and cheese in the haversack, 'He ought to get married.'

'Married?' He looked up. 'What's that got to do with it? It's a good year he wants, not another millstone.'

'Millstone. I like that. You're twice the man since we got married.'

He bent his head over his plate, 'Well, someone had to make an honest woman o' you.'

'Mannie Fairbrother! I'll buy myself a new dress for that.'

The dogs were waiting outside the door, the Jack Russell to go in and the Collies knew it was time to start work.

'Right you two, let's go get them sheep on the move and no loafin' about.'

They raced in front of him through the vegetable garden, leapt the stile into the field and barked impatiently for him to hurry.

The day was a marvellous example of after the rain the sun, the stationary clouds high, white and unmenacing. The swallows darted and swooped sometimes perilously close to the ground and far above the earth a formation of ducks were making for the Arctic breeding grounds. Everything was living again with the spring in full season and nothing living so enjoyable as Mannie Fairbrother.

Taking short thrusting strides he climbed after the dogs up the steep slope. It was not far to where the sheep were penned, a few hundred yards and from around the shoulder of the hill he could hear the lambs. Maybe the lambing had not been good but he would see that those in his care made good meat. Knowing more about sheep than Alan he could feel for his boss who was depressed by the way things had gone. Several of the ewes had aborted and three of the lambs had succumbed to pulpy kidney and had to be slaughtered.

When he reached the hill shoulder and looked into the pen he stopped for one instant, then started to run. Five of the ewes were down on the ground in the stiff attitudes of death. He went in closing the gate, had a look at the dead sheep, hung his haversack on the gatepost as he left and broke into a loping run.

'Where the hell is he?' Alan Barnes was standing at the gate of the pen and, as he watched, a ewe had a violent convulsion. His anger was not at Jim McConnachie who would come as soon as he got the message but at the unplayable hand he was being dealt that year.

Mannie had first telephoned the vet who had been out on his rounds and Paula had assured him she would keep trying the farms until she caught up with him; then he had rung Lane End farm and Alan had been out repairing a broken gate. It was now almost noon and as the ewe contorted with a second convulsion another one on the far side of the pen had a spasm of jerking. Frustrated by his helplessness he saw the first affected ewe collapse and turned his back on them. That was when the vet's cap bobbed into sight over the hilltop, followed by the shorter Mannie's.

Jim McConnachie had a respect for these hill farmers that had grown from seeing them take repeated hammerings from the weather and disease over a period of forty years. Rarely did any of them throw in the towel and seek an easier way of earning a living, and the most typical of them he likened unto unsinkable ships. But the toughest, most durable of them were not entirely immune from suffering some degree of depression and it was as important to Jim to do what he could for them as for their animals. Not physically with medicine but with a sort of bedside manner calculated on the spot to suit the needs of the moment. He knew all about Alan's troubles, that this farmer's bad luck had lasted too long for the bluff, hail-fellow approach, that here a show of quiet, very sure confidence was needed.

With a wordless nod Alan opened the gate for him and with the same salutation Jim went into the pen. His examination was quick and thorough and with a question on his face Alan opened the gate for him to come out. Jim smiled.

'I'm just popping down to the car, nothing to worry about, you're not going to lose any more.'

Alan started to ask a question and closed his mouth. Jim was already striding purposefully away.

'What d'you reckon? he asked Mannie instead.

Mannie took the haversack from his shoulder, took out the flask and filled the cap with tea which he offered to Alan. 'I'm buggered if I know. But Jim does. You could see he knew straight away. Have a sup o' tea and take his word for it. It's going to be all right.' They drank in turns from the cup until Jim came back ten minutes later carrying a wooden box. They carried on sipping, doggedly

123

silent as Jim filled a hypodermic syringe and injected the collapsed ewe. Deftly then he went on to treat the whole flock and carried his box from the pen with a smile of quiet triumph.

'I hope you've not drunk all the tea.'

Mannie gave him what was left in the flask and the three of them stood leaning on the gate.

'What's wrong with 'em?' Alan asked.

'Oh, nothing more than calcium deficiency,' Jim answered airily with mental fingers crossed that it was calcium deficiency and not the rarer, but not unknown, lack of magnesium. The second possibility was also easily cured but Jim wanted to give Alan the lift he would get from hitting the bull's-eye first time. And his diagnosis was accurate. He always got a kick from the wonder on the faces of shepherds and farmers at the speed with which the simple treatment worked. In a few minutes the ewe got to its feet as if it had only been asleep and miraculously the flock was again healthy with the lambs jumping stiff-legged or bleating for milk.

'Well,' Alan shook his head, 'I don't

know how you do it.'

'Nothing at all,' Jim grinned, 'when you're a genius it's—' Mannie hooted, 'Hey up, Alan he's after another couple o' pints.'

'And he's welcome to 'em if he can win 'em at darts.'

'That's how much you're appreciated round here,' Jim told the flock.

Alan carried the box back down the hill when they left Mannie to take the sheep to the grazing, 'What's the cause of this calcium deficiency?'

'Can be a few things. It comes on quite often if they're badly frightened. Don't ask me why, it just happens.'

'You mean like a fox among 'em or something?'

'Could be, but they're so easily scared it could be just anything that startles them and, of course, that might not be the cause at all.' They both refused the lunch Brenda wanted to make them, Jim to get back to his broken round and Alan to his gate mending.

The taproom of the Spotted Dog Inn was classless and popular. It was built seemingly in the middle of nowhere between Thirsk and Sutton, but the landlord used the magnet that will draw drinkers for miles, risking the breathalyser and heavy heads: he served a pint of beer that was unbeatable.

In the Spotted Dog professional men, tradesmen and labourers were given the same welcome provided they possessed twenty-eight new pence or even fourteen to buy a half pint. Graham and Freda Maxwell were regulars and were wedged into an alcove seat with faces flushed by more than laughing at bawdy jokes. They were with their regular company, friends of longstanding who cared nothing for ceremony or etiquette. An empty pint glass was thumped down noisily in front of Graham with another two on its heels.

'What's up,' asked an old farmer with a face of brown elephant hide, 'as she sewn thi' pockets up or summat?'

'All right, all right, give me a chance,' Graham protested. 'Anyway, I can't get out.'

'You can now,' grinned a retired builder who had come to live at Kilburn.

He shuffled out sideways, taking his stool with him and leaving a narrow passage.

'And don't be having a quick one on your own at the bar,' Freda warned him.

The farmer's leathery jowls swung as he laughed, 'Give over, 'e'd be payin' twice then.'

Graham sidled round the table, collected the empty glasses and tacked through the crowd to the bar. It was ten minutes to closing time and he had to queue two deep, ready to jump his place when he got the chance. A very tall thin man came to stand next to him, a man dressed in old clothes with a muffler knotted at his throat. His occupation according to his income tax returns was odd job man and officially he made a very poor living. Unofficially those in the know could buy game birds, rabbits and hares at much more favourable prices than those asked by butchers and poulterers. Pecker Johnson's subsidiary trade was an open secret. He was very good at it, two near misses were the closest he had come to being caught and general opinion held that that was the closest the law would ever come to getting him in the dock.

He nudged Graham, 'I'ear tha's lookin' for a dog.'

Graham did not exactly dislike Pecker and he certainly had nothing on which to base hatred but he was always suspicious of poachers, of the methods they used in snaring and killing. How could they take the time and trouble to be humane, he asked?

'I am, a Lurcher, we lost it a couple of days ago, have you see it?'

'No, but I know where it's 'olin' up. There's part etten rabbits all overt' place.'

Graham grinned, 'Pinching all yours, is he?'

'Not much longer 'e isn't. If you don't catch 'im, I will.'

'Where is he?'

Pecker gave him the exact location of Juttal's cave and offered, 'I'll give you a 'and if y'like. If we miss 'im my Nobby won't.'

Pecker's Nobby was a fearsome Dobermann/Alsatian cross, loyal and obedient to his master but a dog that other dogs, and men, would walk around if they were wise.

'No thanks, we'll catch him if he's there.'

''e's there. If yer go just after dark 'e'll be feedin'. Gone wild, I reckon.'

'Thanks for letting me know—Three pints o' bitter and three halves, please.'

Juttal lay outside his cave, on his side at full stretch asleep. The ledge was a perfect sun trap in the afternoons and after a long trip of exploration to the north that morning he slept deeply, his facial muscles twitching with his dreams.

However free a life is lived, that life must fall into patterns of some description. The patterns may be loose, repeated only at long intervals but the regularities will be there because man is a creature of habit. The design of a life lived in a city will move in a tight orbit around the axis of factory or office from the starting and finishing point of the home. The daily horizons of the Romany are much broader, based on the seasons and ancient horse fairs. Nevertheless, within the main outline of this apparently unfettered life-style necessary routines must exist. And through time dogs have acquired some of the ways of living of the men who own and dominate them. They have become addicted to habit and when Juttal's were taken away from him he quite naturally and instinctively started to form a new set for himself.

He loved to be out and about in the early morning when the day was sharp and fresh and the diurnal animal world was awakening, when the night hunters were slinking away from the sun. After his brush with the two men down on the road he stayed away from the plain, roaming north, east or south or all three in a big circle, and very quickly learning his way about. None of the men he saw, tractor drivers or field workers, offered to harm him and he ignored them. His philosophy, had he realised it, was live and let live and mind your own business. Home was now his small cave, he could live off the land breaking none of the rules Albert had taught him and he wanted nothing else. He did not know there could be anything else to want. He was happy.

There was one small point of annoyance about his new home. or rather the vicinity it was in, He was seeing more people. The good weather was bringing out the sight-seers and tourists. Many cars ground up the steep hairpin road from the plain to stop in the open space at the top, and up on the very rim of the escarpment he was seeing small groups of people more frequently. He could not know that he had chosen to live in one of the most famous beauty spots of the north, or that the pathway on the rim was part of the Cleveland Way and that in high summer the hikers and ramblers would make a never ending shuttle from north to south and vice versa.

When he woke that afternoon he could hear the voices high above him, the giggling as a pack of Brownies passed. He took no notice. The talk and laughter were not menacing. He enjoyed the lazy equivalent of a human lie-in. On his belly now, forelegs crossed and chin on his paws, he sighed very deeply through his nostrils, comfortably complacent. Only his eyes moved as they followed a bird in flight or a buzzing insect and one fly ventured too close to his reclining head. With a movement so fast it was not even a blur, Juttal's head whipped up, his jaws clicked and the fly was in the first stage of his digestive process. Juttal settled back again.

He stayed there until the shadows of the trees down on the plain were very long and there was the first hint in the air that the temperature was dropping, the time to get up and earn his living. He had a good shake to fluff up his flattened coat, a jaw-cracking yawn, and went north to where the rabbits lived. It was not a worn path he followed but a trail of his own to bring him on the rabbits from the south. Down in the big hollow the lake glinted blackly in deep shadow. Juttal passed behind a large rock and stopped. Planing in from the south was one of the long-necked birds that were good to eat. He tracked its flight down into the shadows, saw the momentary short streak of its wake when it settled on the water and then the dark of its feathers were a good camouflage in the shadow.

Rabbits and birds he had been taught he could take and rabbits were the most accessible, but they went to the back of his mind because fifty yards away was a bird. He turned off his trail to go down, dropped below the last of the sunrays and found it was not so dark in the hollow after all, in fact he picked out the bird at once. It had swum in close to the bank, turning to swim parallel a few feet out. Outrun rabbits, stalk birds. Juttal began to stalk his duck.

He came up quietly from the rear. The duck actually saw him but took no notice, probably feeling safe in its environment. When it did not take flight, carried on its aimless paddling, Juttal kept pace with it, waiting for it to come on to his ground. It did not. It swam on aggravatingly, secure with five feet of water to keep the dog away. The duck was an old one that had been barked at many times when it rested and fed in lakes and ponds and it knew that barking did not hurt, that all dogs do is bark.

So it was taken by surprise when the tantalised Juttal's patience wore out, when the long body hit the water almost on top of it.

Juttal scrambled up the bank carrying the limp duck, dropped it to shake and carried it quickly to the cave. From the ledge he could still see part of the orb of the sun and the light was good enough to inspect his dinner. The art of eating a rabbit he had mastered; this was different, the feathers were not fur that came away with the meat they came away clean from the body with no meat attached. The smaller downy feathers floated about him as he snatched and pulled, blowing and coughing them out until he tired of feathers. He paused with cocked head to look at his duck and there, exposed, was a plump breast. It was his first duck but he knew meat when he saw it. Taking a couple of good sniffs to make sure he started to eat.

Ducks were a messy business, a little bit of rabbit skin went down with the meat unnoticed but these feathers were inedible and had to be cleared away first. The meat was good, though not so plentiful as a big buck provided and he could have eaten more. Not that he was hungry enough to go hunting again but without the heavy drowsiness a big meal brought he did not go into the cave as early as he usually did. He lay outside chewing casually on a webbed foot.

He heard the sound in the very last glimmer of daylight, the crunch of a foot on bracken. Down below a man was climbing the hill through the trees. The webbed foot dropped to the ground, Juttal's head was up, he could hear every footstep.

Graham Maxwell placed his feet carefully, soundlessly, taking his weight slowly with each step. He was nearly panting, breathing slowly and deeply he paused for a rest, leaning against a tree.

It would be full dark soon, the dog would be asleep in the hole with the noose of the dog-catcher in position when Graham shouted to startle him into coming out. He waited ten minutes both to regain his breath and for full darkness. Catching this dog was pure professional pride with him. The animal had been sighted a score or more times in places as far as ten miles away and the farmers were getting worried. The dog had not touched any sheep, there had been no thefts of any kind of stock reported but the farmers were understandably wary of a homeless stray at that time of the year. Whatever happened in the canine mind that turned a dog into a sheep killer might happen to this Lurcher at any time and he would get very short shrift then. An organised hunt with guns. If the dog had to die Graham wanted to see it was done as quickly and painlessly as possible. He took another deep breath. He would see to the dog's fate himself.

He started upward again, as quiet as a plump middle-aged man with no bush training can be, and he thought he was doing very well.

He knew exactly where Juttal's cave was, this escarpment had been part of his playground as a child and despite the years away working in other areas he had not forgotten. The two rocks, the dead tree with symmetrical forks like a giant's catapult and to the left the fox-hole.

He was toiling up the last steep pitch with only yards to go, using his hands, head down, when he heard the warning of the deep continuous rumbling from an angry throat. He stopped. The stars were beginning to come through giving the sky the faintest speckled sheen of silver, enough light to make the silhouette of the dog standing above him, and enough to reflect from the hostile eyes.

Graham's success with animals came from his great faith in treating them kindly. In spite of his previous meetings with Juttal he believed the Lurcher would answer eventually to gentleness.

'Hello, then,' he tried.

He was given the growl.

'No need to be frightened of me, old lad, I won't hurt you. Be a good lad now and let me come up.'

The growl did not deter him, he had the dog-catcher in his right hand, another few feet would get him within range. He would consider getting the dog to the bottom after he was in the bag.

He inched up the slope again and the growl changed its tone as Juttal showed his teeth, it had risen to the whine when Graham dug in his toes and made his cast. He had had lots of practice in the handling of that piece of equipment with properly domesticated dogs used to wearing collars and being led. He had never before tried to catch what was in effect a wild dog, growing wilder by the day—or a dog with such reflexes

Juttal heard the swish of the noose, saw it as some kind of attack, dropped his head and shoulders ready to spring and the noose hit the ground by his paws. His snarl then was chilling as he snapped viciously at the rope, turning back to the man when the rope whisked away. The man was too close to the edge of Juttal's perimeter, the cave and the ledge were his, anyone trespassing must be up to no good.

Still, bred deep into Juttal was the rule that only the area inside the limits was to be protected, warnings may be given to strangers that they were coming close to a danger point but they must not be attacked prematurely. He continued to warn Graham by snarling and showing his teeth and Graham saw he had done this all wrong. No one man was going to take this dog into custody, not with a dog-catcher, and not while it had the advantage of the terrain in its favour. He hated giving up, but there was nothing

138

else he could do. The moment he started down the slope in a scrambling slide the dog stopped snarling. When he reached the first tree it stopped the rumbling and when he looked back the silhouette had gone.

# CHAPTER 5

The following day Juttal went far, farther to the east deep into the Hambletons. The Hambleton range is not as extensive as the Pennines but away from the roads it is sharply serrated by the gills, the steep moorland valleys which are as lonely and can be as treacherous as the Pennines.

He followed the drove-road north to the crossroads, turned right and went on through the hamlet of Merton to Hawnby. He was in the country of the sheep, which were scattered along the roadside cropping the verges, used to traffic and passing people. He ignored them and they ignored him.

He went right again to leave the road and the last trace of man excepting the stone walls, north-east up Blow Gill to Bilsdale Moor, 1,300 ft above sea level with its crystal air and bounding game.

Juttal did not consider why he went there where he had never been before, he considered nothing, led on haphazardly by his fancy of the moment, to dart after a swift green snake and lose it in the heather, to sprint to a hillock after sighting a hare to find it had also seen him and evacuated the spot. There is life everywhere on the bleak moor for those who know where to look. But much as he liked it all, when the sun was halfway down from the zenith he knew it was time to go home for he did not feed and sleep here and he had become fond of his afternoon naps on the ledge outside the cave.

He had not forgotten Albert and the caravan and the horse, they had lived together so long they would never leave his memory, but because he had accepted they were inaccessible to him he no longer yearned for them.

A series of incidents kept him from the road, a diving hawk which had flown with its prey when he got there, another hare that showed as it jumped through a breach in one of the walls. Juttal ran after the hare, which he would not have done had he been able to calculate the long start it had on him and related that to their individual speeds. But he gave chase uphill until it vanished and instead of dropping back to the road carried on along the rolling hill crests.

From the higher tops he could see a long, long way across the heather, over one large area dead and blackened by fire. Beyond that was something else he recognised. A tent. It was a mile away, unattended as far as he could see, and he went to have a look. He covered the last hundred yards very cautiously even though there was neither sound nor scent of anyone inside, going very slowly to look through the loosely tied flap. It was empty—of people, that is.

The bivouac was designed to sleep two and with two people inside there would be little room for anything else. Standing on the groundsheet were two packs that were emitting many smells, the strongest was soap which he did not like, second in strength to the soap was meat and if meat was not actually in the possession of someone or something it belonged to the finder.

It was an old tent with the flaps tied by tapes to the centre pole. These flaps had been tied carelessly with only the middle and bottom tapes and Juttal could easily push his head inside. The soap smell was stronger and so was the meat. With a wriggle he got his forelegs and shoulders in and then it was easy. The soap, he found, was in the first pack and the meat in the second. Both packs had been unstrapped to remove various items lying about that were of no interest to Juttal. He made a start on searching out the meat.

When he put his nose to his pack it toppled over with a clank of metal and he jerked back, bumping into the centre pole. The pack lay still and quiet, he put his nose in again pulling out an assortment of bags and wrappers until his teeth met a soft parcel of steak. The bag was polythene with the neck sealed, the smell and a dribble of blood escaping from a small tear. The few drops of blood on his tongue were tempting, more delicious than any he had tasted before, but his newly-formed habits were becoming ingrained in his system so he would take his dinner home.

Getting out of the tent was not as easy as getting in. The pole was now at a slant and with the parcel in his mouth, he had to shake his head to work it through the flap, and wriggle and heave to get his shoulders out until there was a twang of snapping cord when the tent sagged sideways freeing him.

He dropped the meat to scratch and shake, scooped it up and took off along the hillside with his springy travelling lope. The valley curved to the right, the deep cut banks of a stream dividing it, and walking up the stream as if inspecting it were two young men. Simultaneously as they came into Juttal's sight the tent came into theirs and they lost all interest in the stream. They stood a second, flabbergasted, saw Juttal coming towards them, realised the only thing that could have happened. Shouting angrily they ran up the hill to intercept him, one of them brandishing a tapering pole so Juttal veered to the left uphill until he had passed them, then reduced his speed to the lope.

That they had been threatening him there was no doubt, why they did so he did not know, he could not connect them with the tent and the meat and the incident was another clear example that all men were against him and must be avoided if possible. Experience had taught him that there was only one trustworthy man, and now he was gone it was Juttal versus the world. This was not a strange or improper state of affairs, it was simply the way things were, he hunted rabbits and birds and men hunted him. He had forgotten his latest brush with man before he got home, or rather close to home.

His capture by Jim McConnachie and the attempts of Graham Maxwell had helped to sharpen his suspicion and watchfulness. Even in a short few days he had moved far back in time and his eyes and nose, like those of the fox, otter, badger, never stopped working to pick out possible traps or attackers.

His teeth had gone through the polythene and pierced the meat; the filtering taste was maddening and only the wish to eat at his regular place drove him on. It was just about hunting time when he went over the escarpment lip and for once the rabbits were safe. In the failing light he moved diagonally in as near to a straight line as the going would allow and fifty yards from the cave when he caught the faint smell that should not have been there.

It was a scent he had come across before, the stale pipe tobacco impregnating an old jacket. That the smell came from an aged pipe he did not know or care, but he knew that that scent was only present when a man was close. There was not exactly a breeze, a mere disturbance of the air, and after detecting the first whiff he stood in his track looking, sniffing and listening.

Again a gentle gust carried the obnoxious smell to where he was poised in a clump of bushes and he went slowly to look out from his cover. He could see nothing but stayed where he was when the smell was puffed to him again. He could still see nothing. Then he heard a voice very clearly as Bernard Jackson, uncomfortable and cramped under his bush stage whispered, 'Does tha' think it'll come?'

'He'll come if you keep quiet,' Graham Maxwell replied also in a whisper that carried clearly to Juttal.

The second voice he recognised, he had heard it three times trying to entice him into the dog-catcher and he did not have to see the ambush for that voice to sound the danger bells. If he had been in his cave or on his ledge he would have come out in the open to fight them off, but here, with the men between him and his property, he would play the waiting game until they had gone. And he discovered he was thirsty. Silently he turned about and cut down to the lake.

As always, night came first down in the hollow by the water; in almost total darkness he drank his fill and picked up the meat. He stood there hesitating, wanting to go home, thinking of the men waiting for him. Finally he did the simple thing that came most naturally and set about his dinner down where it was safe.

The shiny wrapping was white, he could see it easily, but it was not so easy to tear it from the meat. It was harder to skin than the duck. When he gripped and

147

pulled the slippy, soft bundle slipped from his paws time and time again, but gradually the small tear lengthened and with a final rive and shake the meat fell to the ground. He snatched at it. It was not as meat should be, it was covered in another thin, clinging skin that he dealt with as rabbit's fur, biting through it and chewing it with the meat. It was a nuisance but it would have needed more than a film of plastic to spoil his enjoyment of his first taste of raw beef. The campers had brought with them two pounds of best fillet steak and if the men waiting at the cave had come up behind him as he ate it is possible they could have got close enough to catch him. The rich, red juices were heavenly, the fine texture of the beef paradise, and his mind was closed to everything but his marvellous feast.

When the last morsel was gone he lay beside the lake watching the first twinkling of the stars, replete, completely satisfied. He stayed there a long time, not with any thought of waiting until the men had tired and gone away but because he was so thoroughly content with his overloaded stomach and in a pleasurable mood of indolence.

When he did get up to go home the moon was high and he went up the slopes at what was for him a plod. As he got closer he tasted the air and he smelled nothing but the sweetness of the greenery and the faint odour of the meat clinging to his lips. The men had gone.

* * * *

Paula McConnachie took the golden brown steak pie from the oven and hung the oven gloves behind the door. When she turned to test the potatoes she nearly tripped over Rufus who could always be relied upon to home in on the scent of food.

'Out, out,' she scolded mildly, 'Go see Fred.' she shooed him into the hallway and closed the door knowing he would stand there optimistically sniffing as long as there was anything to sniff at.

It was seven-thirty, an hour later than they usually ate, but Jim had telephoned to say he would be late. She was straining the cabbage when she heard the car come up the side of the house to the garage, a sign that he had, hopefully, finished for the day. He came in the back door looking tired.

'All done?' she asked

'All done. How's Fred? I'll just take a look at him.' The old Boxer was off his food, listless and disinterested so Jim had left him at home with Rufus to keep him company. As he left the kitchen Rufus sidled in again with what could only be a beseeching look on his big face. She pointed to the door.

'Out.'

Rufus shuffled back one pace and whined.

'Out!'

Bodily he went out to stand in the hallway with his stare fixed on the pie, spiritually he was at the table helping to eat it.

'There's no filling your dog,' she said when Jim sat at the table. 'He hasn't been fed an hour and he's begging for more.'

'Oh, he's my dog again is he? He was yours when he won the dog with the waggiest tail competition at the Show.'

Paula laughed, 'Circumstances alter cases. Is Fred all right?'

'Aye, I've given him something to buck him up, he'll be fine tomorrow.'

'Old age?'

'I reckon so mostly.' Energetically he attacked his meal to take his mind off Fred who had already enjoyed a longer life than most dogs and was perceptibly becoming more lethargic as his great age weighed on him more heavily. She guessed the trend of his thoughts, knew that for all his years of dealing with animals he had not, like many vets and doctors, grown hard and inured. It would be a tragedy for him when Fred's time came even though he knew the worst could happen almost any day.

'What kept you today?' she asked.

He juggled with, chewed and swallowed a piece of hot meat, 'Tis pie's beautiful. I'd to go to Alan Barnes's sheep again. It's a shame for that man, he's such a hell of a worker he just doesn't deserve the luck he's having. Calcium deficiency again, so soon after the last attack but he didn't lose any this time. I think if I was him I'd want to

151

pack it up and go into something else.'

Paula smiled, 'No you wouldn't, you're just as stubborn as he is. And *is* it simply bad luck?'

'Oh, aye, nothing but. He's a good farmer and he's got a grand shepherd in young Mannie. Mind you, it's getting him down and you can't wonder.'

She watched him as he cleared his plate. 'You look tired, why not stay in, have an early night?'

He shook his head. 'I feel fine and I promised Alan we'd see him in the Spotted Dog—and a night out won't do you any harm.'

'It's nearly eight now.'

'We'll be there for nine, we don't go out often enough.'

'I'd better start the washing-up, then. Do you want anything else? There's some pie left.'

'No thanks.' A nose nudged his leg as Rufus presented his begging bowl. 'But there's a lad here who'll see it doesn't go to waste.'

Wednesday nights were the quietest of the week at the Spotted Dog, the reason Jim preferred that evening. Most of the customers were local or fairly local people, mainly farmers who talked a lot of shop.

Alan Barnes with Joan, Mannie Fairbrother with Brenda were a foursome waiting to become a sixsome. Mannie said, 'Jim's late.'

'He will be, havin' to come out to us again.'

'Never mind, love,' Joan consoled him, 'he got there in time.'

Alan grunted, emptied his glass with uncustomary speed and reached up to put it on the bar, 'Two an' two halves o' bitter.'

Mannie grinned, 'Steady on, I haven't got over the other night yet. Ah don't want moanin' Minnie on to me agen in the mornin'.'

'I say them that gets drunk should suffer for it,' said Brenda smugly, 'an' there's Jim an' Paula now.'

'Give us a pint and a half of Peculiar as well,' Alan amended the order.

'Evenin' all,' Jim grinned, 'how much start have you got on us?'

'Not much, we had to wait for waddlin' Brenda to squeeze into a dress,' Alan said as he passed the drinks.

'I'm not that fat yet!'

Paula offered her cigarettes. 'Typical chauvinist remark. *They* ought to have the kids, it'd be a different tale then.'

'Listen at 'em,' Mannie jeered, 'if a daft ewe can have one an' think nowt about it I'm sure I could.'

Joan prodded him, 'That's because ewes *are* daft, we're not.'

'Another matter of opinion,' Jim murmured.

Alan beckoned Mannie and Jim closer, 'Did you hear the one about this bloke who had a dream. He said to his wife—'

'Alan Barnes!' Joan threatened, 'you *dare* tell that one in company.'

The evening went on as such evenings usually did with one exception. Instead of growing merrier Alan became morose and no amount of jollying cheered him up. For once alcolhol was affecting him adversely.

During one of the infrequent lulls in trade the barman came to lean on his side of the bar close to them. He grinned. 'Hey, Jim, have y'heard that dog's

154

latest?'

'D'you mean about Graham and Bernard's wild goose chase last night?'

'No, yesterday up in the gills it pinched two pound o'fillet out of a tent, knocked the tent down an' all. Served 'em right though, they shouldn't have been campin' up there.'

'Up in the gills?' asked Alan dourly.

'Aye.'

'Oh, he's a roamer all right,' Jim verified. 'He's spotted all over the place.'

Alan tossed down the remains of his drink and banged it on the bar. 'And I've a feelin' it's paid Lane End a couple o' visits. Something caused that calcium deficiency and I'll bet it was the bloody Lurcher.'

Jim shook his head, 'Unlikely, I'd say.'

Mannie agreed. 'No sign that he's tried to worry any of the flock.'

'You said yourself anything could scare 'em, it needn't have attacked 'em,' Alan pressed.

Joan emptied her glass and passed it up to be refilled. 'If all the tales are true it's livin' well on rabbits and it's not a young dog; it'll know better than to go near the sheep.'

Pecker Johnson came from the back of the room with an empty glass. He ordered his drink and stood leaning on the bar smiling contemptuously, 'I've never heard owt like it.'

'Like what?'

Methodically Pecker conted his money on to the bar, took a slow deliberate drink, 'All this messin' about over a dog. Why don't y' just go out and catch it—or shoot it.'

'It hasn't been shot because it hasn't done anything terribly wrong yet. It's only trying to survive. Graham'll have him soon.'

'Graham?' Pecker scoffed, 'Tell 'im not to forget 'is kid gloves, he'll be messin' about till Christmas.'

Paula snapped, 'Graham's a good man at his job. He knows what he's doing.'

'S'matter of opinion. An' I'll tell you summat else, most'll agree wi' me when that Lurcher's done some real damage.'

'And I think it's done enough already.'

156

'Now, Alan,' Jim said quietly, 'you're blowing it up out of proportion. The Lurcher's a trained guard dog and he'll defend his own, true, but he's passed this way many a time and never caused any trouble. It's the position he's in now, he doesn't know what to do. And Graham's going out after him again tonight—he might have him in the bag by now. I hope so.'

Pecker picked up his drink, challenging as he went back to his seat:

'I've a tenner that sez he hasn't.'

Joan, with the help of the other women, eased the conversation away from Juttal and the crimes he was expected to commit, but Alan's contributions were no more than half-hearted with his mind very much somewhere else.

The subject came up again at 10.25 as Mannie was ordering the last drinks. Graham Maxwell entered pulling off a donkey jacket. His trousers were dirty and a piece of twig was sticking from the top of his turned down wellington boot.

'Just in time,' he said wryly. 'I'll have two, I could drink the brewery.'

Graham's face told Jim he had been

157

wise not to accept Pecker's ten pound bet but he asked, 'No luck?'

'Only bad. Y'know, if I didn't know better I'd swear that dog's psychic. It must have a nose like a Bloodhound.'

He sat down to light a cigarette and take the first relaxing drink. Alan asked him what had happened.

Juttal had enjoyed his normal routine that day, off exploring in the early morning and back for his nap in the afternoon. He had not been lucky enough to come across any unguarded and therefore unowned meat but he had been unmolested, in fact he had seen very few people. He had chased another hare for fun and had tried to spring on several birds, but with no cover to use they beat him into the air by yards.

After his snooze he went to take a rabbit from the regular burrow and his previous success was his undoing. He approached too confidently and carelessly, they heard him coming and were safely underground. He had to go a fair way to the north to come on a lone rabbit, a really big buck, so intent on feeding with its back to him that it was an easy kill. It had not quite got into its stride when Juttal's jaws snapped off its life.

He was almost home when he caught the scent of man, not the same pungent odour as the previous evening. This was more subtle, natural, but just as unmistakable.

He stopped dead to sniff and listen. This man made no sound and without the aid of his keen nose Juttal would have walked into the trap. As it was his nostrils did not let him down and stealthy men always conjured up a picture of the dog-catcher. Silently he turned and made his way down to the lake where no one had ever tried to interfere with him.

'...so you see, there's evidence all over the place that he's still living there but does he ever show up when I'm waiting?'

'Poor Graham,' Brenda laughed, 'two wasted nights.'

'Not wasted,' he contradicted, 'I know I'm going to have to pull something special out to catch that feller.'

Paula laughed, 'I think you are

enjoying it, Graham Maxwell, modern man against the primitive.'

Alan, still despondent, found nothing amusing about it. 'It's all right for you lot that haven't got a flock to worry about. But I'll tell you this, I'm taking the gun to work with me and if I see it it won't bother anybody else.'

Pecker took his glass back to the bar before leaving, grinning sardonically, 'What you been tryin' to cop that Lurcher wi', Graham, baby talk an' chocolate? Y'should 'ave 'ad it easy up in that old 'ole.'

'I'm using a standard dog-catcher and I'll get him with it. What do you suggest, a gin trap or something equally humane?'

Pecker had full confidence in his knowledge of animals and their behaviour. He was, in effect, a hunter and his line of thinking was more direct and drastic than Graham's. 'Whatever I use I'll back meself for twenty quid I can catch that dog afore you. In fact I'll make the same bet I can 'ave 'im dead or alive inside two days.'

'I'll do it my way.'

Alan said seriously, 'I don't care who gets it as long as someone does before it costs me any more vet's fees.'

'I've told you, Alan—'

Pecker broke into Jim's protest, 'I'll tell you what, Alan, if it's worth a tenner to you I'll fetch it in in any case. Just to do you a favour.'

Alan hesitated fractionally, then nodded, 'You're on, get it before it scares my sheep again and the tenner's yours.'

'Now Alan—' Graham started but Pecker grinned.

'Right, it might be on your doorstep when y' get up in the mornin'. Goodnight all.'

He left before Alan could change his mind.

Juttal left it late before he went home again and when he did the man had gone. He did not go to sleep at once despite the very satisfying meal the buck had made. He was vaguely uneasy at all the attention he was suddenly getting from men. He had up to then never been disturbed in the night but still the warning instinct told him to be careful, that extra sense that is vital for self preservation in the wilds but which man, in his civilised way of life, has discarded.

He lay listening to the noise of the vehicles going up or down the road, a distant sound that carried clearly in the still night. If he had looked out he would have seen the sweeping headlight beams raking the sky but moving vehicles did not concern him. When all the traffic had gone he listened to the more natural night sounds, the rustlings and hootings, a quick rushing as something pounced.

Then he heard another vehicle that stopped dead, he heard the slam of a door and that did not bother him either. A few minutes later he heard something that did, a crackling snap as someone walked on bracken. It was not in his immediate vicinity but he left the hole and went to watch from the ledge. He could see nothing.

The scuffling as someone scrambled up a slope was closer and that was followed by a long silence. So long that Juttal turned to go back inside when the branches of a bush were knocked together by a passing body. He could see nothing down in the black shadows of the trees and undergrowth but he knew for sure now that there was someone or something large coming nearer.

He picked out the man first as he stepped softly from the cover of the trees into the starlight, a tall thin man with a big dog walking at heel. Slowly they crossed the narrow stretch of level ground to the last slope leading up to the ledge and the dog growled a very low warning. The man stopped and stared up. When he made out Juttal's shape he dispensed with stealth. He stood there with his dog sitting at heel and spoke in a not un-friendly way.

'It looks as though y've got all your chairs at 'ome, lad. If y'd stayed asleep inside we'd 'ave 'ad you easy as you was comin' out. We'll still 'ave you as it is but it's goin' to be 'arder on you, that's all.'

Juttal stood silent, looking down. The intruders had not crossed his boundary yet. The man took a small bottle from his pocket, unscrewed the cap and drank as Albert used to. He stopped the bottle, put it away and wiped his lips, 'Aye,

163

you're worth a tenner to me, but it's not just the brass, I suppose some'd call it professional pride showing the RSPCA feller how to suck eggs. I 'ope y' come fairly quiet, 'Eel, Nobby.'

When the man started forward again the dog was glued to his left leg and he took out a plastic muzzle and a chain choker collar fastened to a piece of thick rope.

Juttal started to warn them when the man took the first long step up the incline, the dog working its way up with short measured bounds, maintaining station by the man's side. When they were halfway up Juttal was snarling with hackles up and teeth showing. The man grunted, 'Y' can make all the noise y'like, y'comin' wi' me just the same.

Pecker would have preferred the simple way, catching Juttal asleep and getting the muzzle on as he came out but Juttal's awareness and show of anger was no deterrent. There was another way of muzzling him just as sure. He was convinced he had the fiercest, strongest fighting dog ever in Nobby and while Nobby held Juttal he ought to be easy to muzzle, then the chain around his neck and the money was earned.

As Pecker climbed he kept his eyes on Juttal to gauge how far he would let them approach and he got the distance right to the inch. When Juttal crouched with bunched haunches Pecker stopped and crouched, turning Nobby bodily until he was facing to the left at right angles to their line of approach. At the order 'Away!' Nobby trotted off in the 'sendaway,' moving from his master in a straight line for five yards when he instantly obeyed the order to sit. Now they were a triangle with Juttal at the apex still crouched and snarling. Pecker took another quick swig from his bottle watched by both dogs, Nobby awaiting the next order. Pecker reasoned that it would be over in seconds. He would send Nobby in to engage the Lurcher and he himself would be at the top in five more strides. Nobby would disengage as soon as he was told and the Lurcher would suffer a minimal amount of injury.

Where Pecker went wrong was in calculating Juttal's priorities, thinking his attention would be diverted to the attacking Nobby, but Juttal saw only the man as a threat. The first flash of action took seconds.

Pecker pointed at Nobby, swept his arm to aim at Juttal and snapped, 'Fetch him!'

As his dog started bounding upward he made his mistake in going in almost simultaneously himself. Juttal was still watching him and as he crossed the boundary with the obvious intention of gaining the ledge Juttal jumped down to attack him. Two steps and Juttal leapt at Pecker's face, Pecker raised his arms, took the bite on the elbow, fell backward and rolled down the slope with Juttal snarling horrifically and snapping his big yellow teeth at the poacher's face. Pecker had him by the throat to hold him off and they had not reached the level when the shadow of Nobby's body thudded into them.

Throughout the escarpment curious heads were raised in nests and dens by the sound of the fight. As soon as Nobby came to his aid Pecker let Juttal go and rolled clear, his elbow numb, his forearm and hand tingling with electric pains, but he was singleminded, flexing the life back into his hand as he searched for the muzzle and choker.

Juttal had been spoiled in a way. His many, many fights with other dogs had always been brief with his opponent fleeing in yelping retreat, but this first cross of two renowned fighting breeds was different. Bulkier and heavier than himself with just as much heart and stamina, Nobby fought back with a fury to match Juttal's. The dog that bit Pecker bit Nobby, the dog that bit Juttal imperilled himself, a situation that could only result in the irresistible force meeting the immovable object.

Neither animal gave a thought or even recognised pain as they battled across the narrow level ground with Pecker dancing round them trying for the instant he needed to whip the muzzle on. He did not get it.

Juttal's agility counterbalanced Nobby's superior strength and it was the classic contest of skill and speed meeting brawn but there was nothing defensive in the match. It was all-out attack on both sides as they charged, crashed, fell,

167

tumbled to the edge of the second slope. Twisting quickly, Juttal lunged and got his teeth into the side of Nobby's neck, Nobby snarled like a mad demon, rearing up to pull away, and they both went over the edge. Juttal let go his hold when he felt himself turning over in the air. Separated they cartwheeled down the ten-foot slope at an angle of forty-five degrees, Juttal scrambling to his feet and Nobby lying stunned at the base of a tree, Pecker came sliding down after them and Juttal had accomplished his task of driving them away from his home. His red rage died as quickly as it had sprung up. The other dog was lying whimpering in a daze and the man was bending over him. There was nothing else to do here. Juttal went home.

He felt it on his first upward step, the stabbing pain the length of his left foreleg and the throbbing in his throat. It was hard work hobbling up the hills, he had not regained his breath from the fight and he flopped panting on the ledge to lick at his leg. Blood was oozing from teethmarks above his paw and he licked away for a long time before it stopped.

The soreness of his throat and neck got worse but he could not lick that and it was difficult to swallow.

He could hear Pecker talking anxiously to Nobby, then the noises of them passing through the bushes as they went away. A car door opened and slammed, the engine started, the headlights see-sawed as the car was turned around on the narrow road and when its engine sound had faded into the distance there were only the night noises that should be heard. Juttal went into the hole. It had been a tiring day.

The smooth scream of a low-flying gull woke him and he knew it was late by the height of the sun. There seemed to be a large lump of something blocking his throat that he couldn't swallow away, the cords of muscle on the right side of his neck were stiff, making him wince when he put his head down to lick his paw. The deep holes had bled in the night, streaking his hair, and with his stiff neck it took a long time to clean away the blood.

His wounds apart he was content again now that he had repelled the intruders as

169

was his right—his duty according to Albert—and he could not foresee that men would come again to catch him, that man is adamant about who shall live where and how, that he was looked upon as a greater danger than any other wild animal even though he had never shown the slightest sign that he would molest or steal any of the things he had been taught not to. And because he knew none of this he was happy again.

Neither did he know what a superb animal he was with his speed, his strength, his fine all-weather coat and the perfect health glowing from his eyes. Fortunately for him Albert had been a great lover of meat and his diet had been very close to the original natural diet of a dog, solid flesh. It had built in him the stamina his outdoor roving life had fortified, and his resistance to pain, his recuperative powers were enormous.

He was not troubled by theories that to walk on his injured paw might compound the injury and make it really serious, his throat and neck were annoying but nothing more. There was no reason why life should not go on as normal; it was boring lying in the cave in the daytime so he came out, had a painful shake and set off on his tour.

Limping, sometimes hopping on three legs, he climbed the escarpment by taking the easiest line, pausing for a drink halfway up and went north along the drove-road.

Not long after he started out, Graham Maxwell stood with Jim McConnachie on the ledge looking ruefully at the deserted cave.

'Psychic,' he said shaking his head, 'I told you the damn thing's psychic.'

Jim laughed at him, laid down his dog-catcher and lighted a cigarette. He sat on a small rock. 'Let's just have a minute before we go down.' He poked at the debris scattered along the ledge. 'It looks as though he's eating well, anyway. Rabbits.'

'And a duck.'

'He must be some dog; what a pity he hasn't got a proper home.'

Graham kicked the chewed up webbed foot over the edge. 'It is, but I reckon he's a bit old to settle with anyone else, specially after the life he's lived.'

'Not too old to fight, though. God he made a mess of Pecker's dog and I thought that could beat anything on four legs. Poor beast, I gave Pecker some tongue I can tell you in the surgery this morning. I think he's a bit chastened, though, he won't be so quick with his challenges in future...Fourteen stitches altogether and a lump like an egg on his head.'

For a few moments they were silent, gazing at the incomparable view. Then Graham said softly, 'We could try.'

'Try what?'

'To domesticate this dog when we catch him. I suppose anything's possible with animals and he just might settle down.'

'I doubt it, but I'm with you. But we're going to have to nab him quick, you know how the stories snowball and people that haven't seen him seem to think he's a wolf or something.'

'And he's as good as dead if any of the farmers get him in their sights. Alan's stirred it up a bit, he's been a bit hysteric-al about it if you ask me.'

'Aye, but it's understandable him not

wanting to take any chances on any more mishaps. Let's go home and get down to business about how we're going to catch this dog in time.'

# CHAPTER 6

As Juttal went over the crossroads and on to where the drove-road dwindled to the same unpaved track the herds had trod, Alan Barnes was driving west from Helmsley along the A170. He was coming from an unsatisfactory hour with Joan who had taken him to task in a gentle way about his silly behaviour the previous evening in the Spotted Dog. She had tried to make him see he was wrong to allow himself to get so worked up over the stray. It was not like him, he *was* being hysterical, out of character.

They had not fought about it, it was more of a discussion and it had altered nothing. Admitting it was not a hundred per cent certainty that Juttal had scared his sheep, he insisted the probability was very high and no one could argue against the dog having to go at all costs. The longer it remained at liberty the more likely it was it would turn to sheep worrying.

He rounded a sharp bend and saw a small green van coming towards him. He flashed his headlights, slowed and parked with his nearside wheels on the verge. The van did the same and Pecker Johnson lowered his window, so that they could talk quite comfortably across the narrow road.

'How'd you get on last night?' Alan asked.

Pecker scowled. 'Bloody lousy, my Nobby'll be laid up a week or more an' I can 'ardly bend me elbow. That Lurcher must o' been fed on lions or summat, it's like a soddin' tiger.'

'It beat Nobby?'

'Nearly bloody well killed 'im. Jim McConnachie did 'is nut wi' me this mornin'. I'll tell y' summat, though, I'll 'ave that dog sooner or later, I will that! It's a real 'un, some 'ud say it's too old to train but I'll show 'em.'

'You can't want to keep it!'

'By 'ell, don't I!'

Alan put his hand on the window handle, 'Well you'd better be quick. I've got the gun on the back seat an' Mannie's takin' one with him now.'

'I'll be quick all right, I'm just off to borrer some tackle off a mate o' mine, that Lurcher'll be tied up in my yard by tomorrer mornin'.'

'Not if it goes near my flock it won't.' Alan put up the window and drove on. Pecker came slowly off the verge and went east with his foot hard down. He wanted to own Juttal very badly.

Pecker was uncouth, rough and ready, practically illiterate, all facts he would not have denied, and many people would have said he was uneducated. But there are many areas of education and he was very learned about the trapping of birds and animals and evading the law, also about training and handling dogs. He had in his younger days enjoyed training dogs up to the high standards of the highest grade for working dogs: Police Dog. That is not to say his dogs were used by the police who are very capable of training their own canine constables.

One of the major organisations for dog handlers is the Associated Sheep, Police and Army Dog Society with branches all over the country where a handler will be helped to train his dog, whatever breed, to Police Dog standard. If a dog can learn all the required exercises and perform them efficiently on command it will be graded Police Dog, be it Great Dane or Yorkshire Terrier. Ranked equally with Police Dog is the grade Tracking Dog but privately Pecker thought the former was superior. He still trained his dogs seriously although he no longer entered the working trials, and he knew he could put Nobby through his paces at any time and win a Police Dog certificate, as he could have done at any time since Nobby was eighteen months old.

The attraction Pecker saw in Juttal was a massive challenge. Experienced handlers buy their dogs as pups and start the training at the age of three months. This way the dog becomes trained without realising it, a major point of dog psychology. It is taught to treat the lessons as a sort of game so that it enjoys retrieving, searching and tracking. Obeying orders is the way of life from puppyhood and the dog knows nothing else.

What the handler doesn't know in those early stages is how the dog will act when it is expected to be violent, to bring down a running 'criminal'. It is a fallacy that all dogs will bite. Many dogs will *not* bite and the number of Alsatians rejected by the police for this flaw in character greatly outnumbers the acceptances. And having taught the dog to bite there is the even harder lesson of teaching it to stop on the command, and many dogs are rejected for this.

In his short, sharp brush with Juttal Pecker had seen both qualities. The Lurcher had attacked in earnest when threatened and had retired after disposing of the threat, the perfect temperament in Pecker's eyes. What an achievement it would be if he could take that middle-aged animal and school him into an obedient working dog. He knew many top handlers who would say it was impossible, that Pecker was living in a dream world and fantasising on his undoubted skill, but Pecker had always believed that any dog with good intelligence was trainable at least to a certain extent. He would use every trick in his large repertoire to get the Lurcher's affection. There was no doubt at all that he would catch him. He had said more than once, 'If y' can't out-think a dog, you're not much cop.' And that is all successful dog handling is, outthinking the pupil.

Pecker drove eastward as far as he could go, parking the van by the fish filleting sheds on the pier at Scarborough. In the game season when he delivered pheasants to one of the unscrupulous restaurant owners he dealt with he always brought an extra brace for a fish merchant who was not too fussy about the source of his table birds, and Pecker would take home a parcel of prime North Sea cod and haddock.

Juttal's paw was aching badly as he limped home in the sunset. By his standards he had not gone far that day, three miles or so along the drove-road and he had spent the day sleeping in the sun behind a wall. No one had bothered him, no one had seen him and he had seen no one. That was how he liked it.

He went down the escarpment by the route he had used while still living under the caravan, his descent an accident of perfect timing; when he looked over the drop the rabbits had come out to play. He moved back and limped along to where he could jump down to the rabbits' level; nothing of a jump for him but he yelped and fell at the impact of his wounded paw on the ground. He lay there for several minutes licking away the pain and when he went to look around the bush concealing the rabbits they had gone. It did not occur to him to wait silently behind the bush until they thought it safe to come out again. He knew that on the escarpment he was sure to find more.

He did, in a clearing lower down, but his charge was far too slow, even the young ones beating him to their holes. He searched again and came across a pair who had ventured away from the burrow. When they heard him coming they took flight as he knew they would, leaving him as if he were standing. He tried again in the very last of the daylight when he saw a fat old doe feeding and all he got there was a view of her scut as she streaked to safety. Too weary and sore to bother again, he went home hungry, making a painful drink do for his dinner.

His pain did not make him forget to be cautious as he neared the cave. The small warm breeze from the south was right for him and would carry the scent of danger. What his nose picked up he did not recognise as dangerous although it was something he had never come across before, faintly pungent. He had never had his nose close to new sisal rope.

Slowly he hobbled up the last slope and a few yards from the cave he found where the scent was coming from. The rope lay across his path leading up into the darkness above the cave and away down the hill towards the trees. He sniffed it but not suspiciously, out of curiosity, ropes were not harmful. He went to go into the cave, stopping to sniff again. Men had been here at some time in the day, there was something inside that carried the scent, something he could not see in the pitch black.

For a long time he stood there undecided. He mistrusted anything connected with man but when whatever was in the cave did nothing to hurt him he yawned and entered, quickly curling up and breaking a taut cotton thread. Outside there was an alarming rattle as three empty tin cans fell from somewhere above the mouth of the cave followed by a small shower of stones and earth which was in turn followed by something else that hit the ground with a soft thump.

Juttal moved at the first clang of the cans. Hampered by his injured paw in the confined space he came out to run into the net released by Pecker from his hide down in the trees. Juttal would not have known what the net was if he had seen it, certainly not what it was for, but he did know that he was caught in a mass of yielding floods which moved with him whatever he tried to do.

Juttal fought the net as savagely as he had ever fought anything, biting, tearing, trying to charge and tripping, all the time binding himself tighter and tighter. He battled with the net until his legs and body were hopelessly entangled, until he could not even stand up. He lay on his side looking throught the meshes pressing into his face, and in his helplessness came very close to fear, the same fear that cracking thunder gave him because he could not fight it or chase it away. The fear left him, though, when he heard the man coming up the slope. He tried to fight again, to get loose and drive the man away.

The light got to him before the man, the blinding beam hit him in the face and he was so caught up in the net he could not turn away. It bobbed towards him jerkily, jumping away and sweeping back and from behind it came a satisfied laugh. Juttal growled, tried to snap and his snarl was like a howl when the man came over the boundary and walked right up to him.

When the man was a few feet away he stopped, holding the beam steady and examining his catch. When he said, 'You're not in the bag but you're in the bloody net all right,' Juttal knew the voice. He made one last attempt and, defeated again, lay quietly with bared teeth in the cone of brilliant light. He could do nothing else.

Pecker was not in a hurry, he had not

gone to these lengths to give the Lurcher a chance to slip out of his hands by being careless. He squatted down by Juttal's head, pointing the light away and starting to talk. He spoke softly with a gentleness that would have surprised his acquaintances, almost the baby talk he had jibed Graham Maxwell about, telling Juttal all about the new life he was taking him to, the dog he was going to turn him into.

He prattled on for five minutes before reaching out to make the first physical contact. Very steadily he made to put a hand on Juttal's shoulder and Juttal went crazy, twisting, writhing, trying to bite.

Pecker said, 'Aye, y're a wild 'un right enough, but y'll learn 'cos I'm gonna learn yer.' Firmly he placed the flat of his hand on the bucking shoulder, kept it there until the contortions subsided and, when Juttal lay still again, maintained the contact as he carried on talking.

'Are y'beginnin' to see there's nowt to be frighted of? No one's gonna 'arm yer while ever you're Pecker Johnson's dog, 'cos that's whose dog y'are now. After a bit you'n Nobby'll get matey an' then we'll be laughin'. But by 'ell, y've a lot to learn.' He started off Juttal's futile struggling again by running his hand from shoulder to hip, doing it again and again until the mad threshing stopped, and then carrying on stroking and talking.

'Y'makin' it 'ard for me, dog— Dempsey, that's what I'll call yer seein' as 'ow y'can fight—I've got this 'ere muzzle in me pocket but 'ow the 'ell am I gonna get it on. I think if we go off this ledge I'll 'ave a better chance. Let's see.'

Grasping the trailing folds of net Pecker dragged Juttal to the slope and eased the tossing, jerking bundle down to the narrow level stretch by the light of the torch he had jammed in position at the top. It made no difference, whenever he made a new move Juttal started trying to fight, and in the end Pecker stood up to flex his knees, 'I could 'ave done with a bit of 'elp to get you 'ome. Never mind, where there's a will.'

He laid the muzzle down close to Juttal's head, 'There y'are, 'ave a look at it,' and took out a large bladed clasp

185

knife. Taking no notice of the frenzied struggling he knelt astride, holding Juttal's body down with his buttocks and gripping his neck with his knees. The muzzle was the modern kind, in effect a basket of stiff plastic which was fastened by a strap around the neck with enough room when fitted to ensure the dog's comfort, enough even for it to drink.

Pecker pulled the muzzle over Juttal's helpless and still netted head, buckled the neck strap and, with accurate timing, snatched at a moment when the dog's mouth was closed to hold the pointed jaws shut. With Pecker's weight bearing down on him Juttal could do nothing. He kept on trying but Pecker had all the advantages. Carefully Pecker put the tip of the knife through the bars of the muzzle and cut a strand of the net, putting all his power into holding his dog still. He thought of Juttal as his dog now. He worked the length of Juttal's jaw line until there was a hole in the net large enough for his head to come through. He stuck the knife in the ground and began working the net back over Juttal's head, a tricky job inside the muzzle, but he did it. He then took the chain choker from his pocket, slipped it over Juttal's head, enlarged the hole in the net with one slash of the knife and jumped to his feet. Juttal jumped to his. It took a hectic two minutes of wild threshing and jumping to work his body from the rest of the net and when he thought he was free he was not. There was the chain round his neck with Pecker holding very tightly to the rope that was attached to the chain.

The first thing after such close confinement was a thorough shake and the second was to get the restrictive muzzle off. He pawed at it, violently shook his head but it stayed there. He was so anxious to get rid of the muzzle that he forgot Pecker until a sharp tug on the choker pulled him round to the left.

'Heel,' Pecker said sharply, starting the training there and then, and reminding Juttal who was the cause of his troubles. Juttal went for Pecker.

With a quick spring he went for Pecker's face, his mouth open as wide as the muzzle permitted, snarling pure hatred. Pecker knew too much about dogs to be caught unprepared. There are very few occasions when physical force is advisable in the art of dog handling. An ordinary dog reared from a pup by a good handler will quite probably never feel a blow in its entire life. Pecker was the best kind of expert handler and had never had cause to strike Nobby, but Juttal was an entirely different case. He was used to being victor, the boss, and he was going to have to learn that every creature has a master somewhere.

Pecker met the first spring with a sweep of his arm, throwing Juttal over to crash on his side. He came back off the ground with the speed of a squash ball to be knocked the other way. A dozen times, yo-yo like, he bounced back after each aborted try until the message that he was getting nowhere penetrated.

When he stopped the attacks he stood head down, panting, and raised his left fore leg. When Pecker snapped 'heel' and marched away Juttal tried not to go, to dig in his claws, but it was no good. The sharp, hefty snatches of the choker jerked him unwillingly along and when Pecker told him to 'heel' as he turned at right-angles or fully about Juttal was jerked along in his wake.

They made a weird picture in the blazing torchlight: the tall, thin man trying to make a speedy impression on the captive wild dog, to make him see that if he co-operated there was nothing to fear, everything to gain. To some extent he was successful.

Juttal with his game leg and sore throat was not at his physical peak and he tired of fighting impossible odds sooner than he might have done before the fight with Nobby. Now his fury had abated he was feeling the pains again, limping along unhappily behind this first stranger ever to defeat him.

As soon as Pecker saw he was complying, if with very bad grace, to the demand of the choker to keep pace, he halted to tie him to a bush while he gathered the net and the ropes. He kept the talk flowing as he worked. 'There y'are, nowt to it, is there, an' when we get 'ome we'll see what we can do with that leg o' yours,' he chuckled, 'I'm gonna get a rollockin' over this 'ere net but there was nowt else I could do, anyway one o' them fishermen'll mend it in five minutes.'

With the net under his right arm, the torch in his right hand, he led—dragged—Juttal down the escarpment, encouraging him all the time to keep up close to his left leg.

He threw the new into the back of his van saying to Juttal,

'In.'

Juttal backed away.

'When I say in I mean in,' Pecker said sternly, gripping the chain close to Juttal's neck, putting an arm under his belly and throwing him in bodily. He slammed the door and locked it, then carried on talking pleasantly as he started the engine and set off home.

At first Juttal stood looking for a way out. The door was closed behind him and in front, separating him from the man, was a metal grid. It was his first time in a van and he did not like it. There was nothing he could do about it. As the van picked up speed on the country road, he staggered from side to side until he lay down to lick at the pain in his paw and wait to see what would happen next.

The jolting, swaying journey did not

last long. The van slowed, stopped, Pecker got out, got in again and the van moved backwards. It stopped again and the unpleasant engine noise died. Pecker got out, hinges creaked, bolts scraped and the van doors opened. Juttal nearly knocked Pecker down as he shot out to freedom. Pecker let him go, grinning when he heard the barking from inside the house. He went across the yard to open the door carefully and prevent Nobby from getting out. Nobby did not like other dogs in his yard and would have to get used to Juttal gradually. Pecker closed the door and through the uncurtained window the light flooded the yard. He stroked Nobby's head.

'We'll give him a minute or two to see he can't get out, eh?'

Juttal found that out very soon. The yard was enclosed by the back of the house on one side and a high wooden wall on the other three. He made two circuits, paying most attention to the bottom of the wooden walls and hoping to find a hole. There were cracks galore but nothing nearly wide enough for him to get through.

The light was partly blotted out when Pecker appeared at the window to see how he was getting on and the dog Juttal had fought reared up for a look. The dog started to bark angrily but stopped when Pecker said something and put a hand on its head. Juttal did not bark back. He was on strange ground, uneasy, unsure of what to do when there was nothing he could do but wait.

He made another hopeful tour of his prison, the pain making him limp again and when he lay down by the van the house door opened and Pecker came out to him.

He had water in a bucket, deep enough for Juttal to drink through his muzzle. He put the bucket down and stepped back pointing, 'Go on, then, y'must be thirsty.' Juttal was. He was also very suspicious of this tall man who had an answer for everything Juttal tried and he kept his eyes slanted up at the man as he drank.

Pecker had moved away for exactly that reason, knowing that if he was to get 'Dempsey's' confidence everything would have to be above-board from now on.

The dog would learn that his new master could be trusted completely, that there would be no more trickery and one of the most important tests was coming up now. Pecker was going to put to the test his theory that Dempsey would only fight to protect his own or escape capture. In this yard the dog owned nothing and Pecker was going to release him from the muzzle so if the theory was correct Pecker had nothing to worry about. If he was wrong those fangs were long and sharp, the jaws very strong and the dog knew well how to use them. Pecker Johnson was justified in his high opinion of his own knowledge of dog mentality and behaviour but not so cocksure as to think himself infallible. It had been known for the most devoted of dogs to turn on their own masters for some reason, the same reason which can make a loving parent savagely attack his own child. There is no forecasting or accounting for temporary mental aberration and Pecker's assessment of Juttal *was* nothing more than pure theory. He could be an habitual canine criminal. There were many flaws in Pecker's make-up but one of them was not lack of courage.

When Juttal had quenched his thirst he took two limping steps back from the bucket and stood on three legs, his eyes never shifting from Pecker. Pecker did not move at once. He lighted a cigarette, took two long drags and grinned. 'It's all up to you, Dempsey. If y'turn out to be a villain I'll 'ave t' send for Maxwell. If y'don't I reckon we can 'ave a good time together, me an' you an' Nobby.'

Juttal did not move, he made no sound, he just watched cautiously. Pecker continued to talk on all the time and when he thought he had spent long enough on the opening gambit he took a slow, short step forward. Juttal hopped a quick step back, making the chain choker rattle.

'Oh aye,' Pecker grinned knowingly.

The rope he used for a lead ran from the choker to Pecker's left and the end was behind him so he was walking away from Juttal when he went to it and Juttal did not mind his going away. When he started coming back, taking in the slack of the rope Juttal tried to retreat but Pecker's grip was firm, held him steady.

Inexorably he came along the nine feet of rope, hand over hand with Juttal trying to pull away, talking, talking, and stopping when less than a yard separated them.

'Y'see, it's not too bad is it?'

Juttal stared, his upper lip lifting, the start of the rumble no louder than the purr of a cat coming through the bars of the muzzle. This man had treated him as no one had before, tying him in nets, muzzling him, making him go where he did not want, had taken him away from his home in a van, confined him in this place from where there was no escape and now he was coming close again. What other detestable experience was he about to impose?

Pecker understood all that, guessed it would be as much of a fight to get the muzzle off as it had been to put it on. It was what happened immediately afterwards that would decide Dempsey's fate.

In the same friendly tone Pecker told him, 'Now, we've played about long enough, let's 'ave yer.' His actions were controlled, unhasty. He firmly pulled

195

Juttal closer and Juttal started to struggle, not to attack but to escape, the first good sign Pecker wanted to see. Juttal's second tactic was only expected and had to be allowed for. Pecker thrust his hand from behind through the choker, which he flipped off when he had a good grip of the muzzle. And that was when, predictably, Juttal started to fight as, from his view, he was being captured again. He leapt and reared and tried to bite but this long thin man was very strong, keeping a tight hold with his left hand and fumbling at Juttal's neck with his right. Juttal wanted to bite the hands, to send the man packing, to savage and—and then he was away from the man, free of the thing around his head. In the first instant of joy he had a luxurious, unhampered shake and a swift limping run round the yard but there was still no way out. He stood in the middle of the yard, in the yellow light coming from the window where Nobby was. He was nonplussed, just as much at a loss as when the caravan had gone.

He was directly in Pecker's path to the door. Pecker did not walk around but straight at him and it was Juttal who gave way, first backing off and, when Pecker still went straight at him, moving to the side, Pecker went into the house, had a last grinning look at him, and closed the door.

Juttal yawned and, as it was the only option left to him, looked around for somewhere to sleep. In one corner there was a small shed with the projecting roof of an open lean-to, something to sleep under, the perfect place. Under the lean-to were some of the tools of Pecker's cover-up trade, two saw horses and a wooden box, a few planks of wood. There was enough room for him to curl up and relax until sleep came.

It was quiet here compared with the turbulent night life on the escarpment. He heard the scuttle of what could have been a mouse or a rat and that was all, for his presence made the rest of the small inhabitants of the yard extra careful. Sometime later the kitchen light, the point of focus in the yard, went out and then there was nothing to look at so he went to sleep.

A voice woke him, Pecker's voice

from somewhere over the wooden wall. The voice was happy, playful, as he let Nobby romp in the field and threw things for him to fetch, but after a while it went quiet and after going to the bucket for a drink Juttal went back to sleep.

He woke the second time to the grating of the back door lock when Pecker came out. He got up, then, standing defensively as Pecker walked across to him, slinking away along the wall when the man got too close.

'Good,' Pecker smiled, 'good. If I've got it right you'd nowt to eat yesterday and by feedin' time tonight y'll be feelin' a bit hungry, an' no one makes friends quicker than an 'ungry dog an' a feller wi' summat to eat. But first I've to get the van out an' keep you in. I'll show y'what we'll do.' He went back into the house.

He was quite right, Juttal was hungry, not ravenous at that stage but definitely ready for a meal. He was making another search for a way out when Pecker left the house again. This time he was carrying something that was new to Juttal, something that was giving off a delicious smell, a pork sausage left over from breakfast reheated for the scent to travel further. A dribble of saliva ran from Juttal's mouth and his eyes latched on to the meat held openly on Pecker's extended palm. Pecker opened the door of the shed, said, ''Ere y'are, then,' dropped it on the shed floor and stepped a few paces back. The inference was obvious that the meat was being offered to Juttal and, suspicious as he was, he was urged to slink across the yard and accept the gift by a hollow belly and watering mouth.

He slowed down as he got to the doorway, looking from the fat titbit to Pecker and back. His nose drew in the heavenly smell, and his desire for the sausage overcame his distrust of Pecker. He nipped in through the door and buried his teeth in the sausage, so enthralled by the flavour that he did not nip out again at once as he should have done, but stayed in the shed to eat it, spinning round too late when the door was closed, leaving him in the dark. Always with Juttal first things came first and this time it was his mouthful of sausage which he enjoyed enormously before thinking about his latest plight.

It was dark in the shed, the broad daylight filtered greyly through a single filthy pane. There was not a lot of room. Around the space inside the door the junk was heaped to the roof. It was dark, musty and claustrophobic. Luckily he did not have to stay in there long. He heard the yard gates creak open, the van driven a short distance, the gates close again and then Pecker was letting him out into the yard. As he went by quite close to Pecker's legs the poacher said, 'Yer limpin' better this mornin', anyway, must be clearin' up.'

Optimistically Juttal went round the walls again hoping to find a hole big enough to squeeze through, paying much attention to the gates. Pecker called as he went in the house by the back door, 'Keep on lookin', t'exercise'll do yer good.'

The door closed and Juttal was alone, as he liked to be, but caged as he did not like.

The day was boring, with absolutely nothing to do but wander about the limited space or sleep under the lean-to, and he actually got a thrill of excitement when he heard the van park outside the gates. He ran to look underneath but the gap to the ground was too narrow, he had more success peering through the crack between the gate and post. He could see part of the van and the flash as Pecker passed. There was another flash which returned to bark at him until Pecker shouted, ' 'Eel, Nobby.' Nobby went.

Then there was something else to do. Occasionally he could see Pecker moving about in the kitchen as he made the evening meal and every time Juttal went near for a better look Nobby popped up to bark at him only to be told to get down.

The attraction of the window was the smell of cooking food seeping from it. There can be few meats with a more poweful or hunger inducing smell than frying bacon and Juttal knew what that was. Albert had liked bacon. He had not eaten now for almost forty-eight hours, the longest he had gone without a meal in his life until Albert had left him, and his belly was one griping ache which the bacon raised to an intolerable pitch.

Alternately he paced to and fro under the window or put his paws up on the sill to look inside. He could see a bare flagged floor, an old and dirty wooden table with two rickety chairs, Pecker's back as he cooked the meal at the open fire and Nobby lying where Pecker had sent him in a corner. Juttal had never been in a house, never looked inside one, and the only thing in there to hold his attention was the food Pecker was maddeningly messing about with. His jaws drooled continuously, making pools of saliva which spilt over the edge of the sill and dripped to the ground.

He made a squeaking whimper like a pup when Pecker came to the table and, facing him, piled a plate with rashers and eggs that Juttel recognised and various other things he did not. Pecker seemed not to notice him, sitting facing the window he tucked in, making a show of dipping egg yolks with bread and lifting each forkful slowly to his mouth, chewing very deliberately and, more galling still, throwing pieces of bacon rind to Nobby.

In his frustration Juttal left the window to run aimlessly round the yard, pausing for two quick laps at the water bucket and when he got up on the sill again Pecker was wiping his plate with bread. Pecker was not in a hurry, he took his time smoking a cigarette and drinking his tea, glancing at the evening paper and when he did get up he went out of Juttal's sight to return with a large plastic bag. From the bag he took a bloodstained parcel, tearing the wet paper away to reveal two skinned rabbit carcasses. One of them he threw without looking to Nobby, the other he proceeded to joint with sure unhurried strokes of a large knife. Juttal barked, whined, barked again, the fresh pink meat driving his captivity, his hatred of men, his sore paw from his head.

Pecker dropped the joints into the plastic bag, went out of sight again, the door knob rattled and he was there out in the yard with the bag of food. Juttal dropped from the sill to circle him as he casually walked across to the lean-to and sat on one of the saw horses, 'Now then, let's see if we can start makin' owt of yer.'

Juttal had gone as close as seemed safe, about two yards. Pecker said, 'Down!' When Juttal softly whined he tried another command, 'Sit!' And when Juttal did not respond to that he nodded, 'No one's ever bothered to learn y'owt, mebbe it's as well startin' from scratch.'

He dipped in the bag, held a shoulder with ribs attached, waggled it at Juttal, 'Catch.'

Juttal caught it and it was as well the meat was not boneless or he would have tried to swallow it whole. As it was the bones were cracked, crunched and swallowed so swiftly Pecker said, 'Christ, 'appen I should 'ave give yer summat this mornin' it might be days since yer've 'ad owt.'

Of course, Juttal had not had time in his short association with Pecker to develop any degree of respect for the man, he was still very cagey about going too close, but a show of food is guaranteed to stop the mind of any hungry dog from straying and Pecker made the most of it. He had to get through to Juttal that he would not be harmed, that all that

204

would be offered was kindness with no hidden traps.

Juttal's eyes were fastened on the bag, they transferred to Pecker's hand when it moved toward and into the bag and when a plump leg appeared they latched on to that. Pecker opened his fingers and the leg fell between his feet. Juttal started for it, head down, stopped and looked up at Pecker and Pecker was gazing into space over the roof. Two short slow paces, a quick rush in and Juttal was back at his place tearing at the meat.

'That's the idea, you'll see, y've nowt to be frightened of.'

Juttal took the remaining three joints in the same way and with his stomach filling, the pain gone, he bellied down to give the last leg the full mastication rabbit deserved. He swallowed, licked his lips and blew through his nose. That he stayed where he was six feet from Pecker to let the meal digest, Pecker took as an excellent sign, but he did not move from the saw horse. He lighted a cigarette as he sat to chat confidentially.

'I think I'm gonna crack it wi' you, Dempsey, I think we'll be showing 'em a thing or two at the trials. I've set meself summat aimin' at Police Dog but the sky's the limit an' if we don't think big we'll never *be* big. I suppose I'll deserve a round of applause if yer get as far as Companion Dog, talkin' sense, like. But we'll see. We'll make a real start tomorrer—if I'm not still drunk after suppin' Barnes's tenner. Wait while I tell 'em tonight.'

Juttal felt secure so long as Pecker stayed on the saw horse. The instant his new master got up so did Juttal, to lope away to the water bucket. But Pecker went into the house grinning.

# CHAPTER 7

Pecker left Juttal very much to himself, allowing him the run of the yard, keeping Nobby in the house. In the mornings he put fresh water in the bucket and mooched about the yard, casually talking as though they were old friends. It was in the evenings at feeding time that Pecker really tried to make contact.

Juttal's second meal was like the first except that Pecker dropped all the pieces of rabbit between his feet and he was rewarded by the fact that the dog did not think it necessary to retreat so far with each one. The safety margin of two yards was gradually decreased to one and finally merely a token backward step. The third meal Pecker brought out in a bowl, not rabbit but a mixture of chunks of ox heart and liver. He sat in the same place on the saw horse with the bowl between his feet. 'Come on now,

Dempsey, let's see yer get stuck into that, it'll put iron in yer blood.' Juttal was only concerned with putting food in his belly but he did not rush in as this meal was different. It gave off an appetizing healthy smell, but it was different and new situations need sizing up. As Pecker unconcernedly lit up a cigarette and waved to Nobby looking through the window, Juttal darted in and out to snatch a chunk of liver. The liver was good but unlike rabbit it took very little chewing, he had swallowed it before reaching his safety point. He did the same thing again and Pecker laughed, 'Yer like a bloody shuttle.'

The liver was good, and heart was delicious, cunningly cut in smaller swallowable pieces, and by the time he was nearing the bottom of the bowl Juttal had stopped dashing in and out. He stood with his forelegs slightly apart, head down in the bowl, his suspicion of Pecker dispelled, at least for the moment.

With the fourth meal Pecker took the prolonged exercise a stage further. Instead of putting the bowl on the ground, he sat holding it out with his elbows on his knees, very easy and relaxed. This time it was a few minutes before Juttal timidly walked up, made a grab and scuttled away, and this time, too he had scooped up less than a mouthful. This time the grinning Pecker was offering him finely minced meat that had to be lapped at more like water than torn at and chewed like meat. But it was meat, good meat, so tasty that Juttal condescended to eat from a bowl held by the man who had caught him. And Pecker was very pleased with that significant progress.

The fifth and sixth meals were taken in the same way with Juttal coming to him readily without any show of nervousness and Pecker moved the relationship on a stage before that habit became ingrained. He put his hand on Juttal's shoulder.

At the first touch Juttal shied away with a snarl. Pecker sat patiently holding out the bowl, lightly touching the shoulder when Juttal got engrossed in the mince. In the end those tactics worked. On Juttal's ninth evening in Pecker's custody he ate his mince with Pecker all the while slowly brushing a hand from shoulder to rump. With some reason to be self-satisfied Pecker told him, 'An' now we're gettin' somewhere!'

The evening after that Juttal met him at the door at feeding time, crossed the yard with him and tried to get at the bowl before Pecker had sat down.

'Whoa,' Pecker growled sternly, 'steady on, there's summat else first.' From his pocket he took the chain choker now attached to a four-foot leather training lead. He pushed Juttal away, set the bowl on the ground, said, 'Come on, then,' and as Juttal made blindly for it he felt the loop of chain slip over his head. Pecker did it with the usual stroking movement and if Juttal noticed he did not object. His confidence in Pecker's integrity was building rapidly, as Pecker had expected.

Pecker was also prepared for an eruption when Juttal finished eating and realised he was caught again. It was not so bad. When the last gulp was swallowed and he made to move away there was the ratchet clicking as the chain snugged into his neck. He tried to pull away, to fight the chain; it may be that he remembered the uselessness of trying to get away from the iron grip of the thing around his neck as his tantrum did not last long. When he calmed Pecker stood up, and by superior strength manoeuvred Juttal to stand unwillingly by his left leg.

''Eel!'

Pecker stepped off, giving Juttal no time to make up his mind one way or the other, tugging firmly to get him moving, letting the lead go slack as soon as he obeyed. The biggest and most pleasing wonder of that session was that not once did Juttal make any kind of attack—or even threaten one. He did not like it at all but seemed to blame the choker and lead, snapping at them from time to time when his patience wore thin. Round the yard they went for a quarter of an hour, up and down, turning right, left and about and whenever Pecker made a military style halt, a very definite stamping of the feet, he snapped 'Sit!', vertically jerking the lead and pressing weightily with his left hand on the reluctant rump. He would stand a few moments, forcefully putting Juttal back into the sit position

211

when he stood up too soon—which he always did during that first session.

Firm and unbending when Juttal was disobedient or tardy, praising and stroking when, mostly by accident, he did the right thing, Pecker never ceased to encourage him, using his new name. At the end of the fifteen minutes Juttal had the faintest grasp that it was more comfortable to obey the commands quickly than not, but more to the forefront was his dislike of the choker, and Pecker knew he had no chance of getting the dog's undivided attention until he accepted as normal that essential piece of equipment.

An unknowledgeable spectator might have laughed at the performance, at the way Pecker had to work with talk, snapping fingers and jerks on the lead to keep Juttal moving in the right direction, but any competent handler who knew something of Juttal's history would have given Pecker the credit he deserved. Pecker knew quite well the progress he had made and was not far short of being delighted by it, knowing that as his dog grew accustomed to the procedures his attention would be even easier to get and hold. Then the same rapport which linked Nobby's mind to his would start to germinate.

After the final "sit" Pecker flung up his arms, 'Good lad, Dempsey,' he laughed. 'Good lad. Wild dog! Yer about as wild as a day-old chick at t'bottom of yer. I tell yer, we'll show the bloody lot of 'em, me an' you.' He slipped the lead and Juttal cavorted about the yard, stopping twice to shake and once for a quick drink. Pecker let him have a couple of minutes and tried something else. He went in the house for a moment.

'Dempsey!'

No acknowledgement.

'Dempsey!'

He was ignored again and would be until Juttal learned his name so he went to the mountain. He cornered Juttal by the gate, offered something on the palm of his hand, something with a sweet attractive smell.

'Go on, take it.'

Juttal stretched his interested neck another inch but would not take it.

Meeting him halfway Pecker put it on a stone between his feet, 'Go on, y've earnt it.'

Juttal came forward, sniffed it, tasted it with his tongue and bit it. His teeth went through a thick hard coating into the chewy centre that was a cocktail of delicious flavours all new to Juttal. He bellied down with closed eyes, jaws working contentedly as he enjoyed his first Mars Bar and Pecker left him to it.

Next morning, very early before the sun, Juttal woke up to hear Pecker telling Nobby to get in the van which was parked outside the gate. He ran across to see what was going on only to see the glow of the lights coming under the gate fade away as the van drove off. He went back to bed under the lean-to.

It had been daylight for perhaps two hours when the van came back and when Pecker came into the yard by the back door Juttal sensed his cheery triumph, but did not know that this was generated by the money in his pocket which came from a butcher who was not against buying cheap rabbits in the early hours.

Pecker had to corner him to put on the

lead, but when he had done so he opened the gate and took him outside for the first time. It went to Juttal's head, the fields and trees and, blue-grey in the distance, the escarpment. He tried to bound about for sheer joy of being outside the wooden walls, which Pecker allowed him to do only to the extent of the lead, and not for long at that. They had come out on business.

They went into the fallow field alongside the house and straight into a training session with the introduction of another exercise, Juttal staying put in the sit position.

Allowing for the dog's high spirits at being in the open again the lesson was satisfactory. He co-operated partially when he was not watching the flight of a bird or snapping at some winged insect. He did well enough to earn another reward. They had a short tug o' war in the gateway when Juttal showed his resentment at going back into the yard but it was quite natural and he did not get a black mark. What he did get when the gates were fastened was a large white knuckle bone to gnaw on, an occupation that kept him busy all the time Pecker and Nobby were away repairing a leak in Jim McConnachie's garage roof.

'How's the Lurcher?' Jim came out to ask.

Pecker brought two broken tiles down the ladder, ''e'll be all right when I've knocked a bit o' sense in 'im.' Which was the kind of answer Jim expected and knew to be the opposite from the truth. Whatever methods Pecker Johnson used to earn—or steal—his living, it was certain the Lurcher could not have fallen into better hands.

There was another innovation that evening. After the second training session with a dinner of whole rabbit as a reward, Pecker came into the yard again. He had the lead with him and he left the back door open. Juttal tolerated the lead now, knowing it was harmless, and stood for it to go over his head. Pecker took him under the lean-to, sat on the saw-horse and shouted:

'Come, Nobby.'

Nobby came running out obeying the recall and Pecker dropped him flat in the middle of the yard.

216

'Nah then, you two, yer gonna 'ave to get matey sooner or later so it might as well be sooner. 'Eel, Dempsey—stay, Nobby!' Nobby had taken the order to heel as directed at himself but he dropped again.

This was the only part of the planned programme to educate Juttal which Pecker was now unsure of. Nobby was a possessive dog, not taking kindly to canine visitors, and the few people who came to see Pecker at home wisely left their pets in the car. Pecker had left Juttal out in the yard so long to let Nobby absorb the idea that he now lived at the cottage too. When the two dogs had fought Juttal had been protecting his own and Nobby had been protecting Pecker; they were both doing either what they had been taught or what came naturally. Pecker was hoping that under the new circumstances they would be able to get along together.

Talking reassuringly to them both he took Juttal slowly across to get acquainted with his new running mate. They had eyes, somewhat cautiously aggressive eyes, only for each other. With a rumble of a duet they sniffed at noses and muzzles, and when the rumbling died away Pecker grinned, 'That's the idea, lads.' He slipped Juttal's lead, 'Up, Nobby.'

Left to themselves they really sniffed each other, covering every inch from head to rump. Quietly Pecker went back into the house to watch from the window. Nobby broke it off first by going to the bucket for a drink and as he made a tour of inspection of the yard—his yard that he had been kept from—Juttal had a shake and walked up to the open door. It had never been left open and unattended before.

He looked inside, sniffing at the old odours of cooked food and the conglomeration of smells the kitchen of a none too hygienic householder acquires, some smells good, some not so good, all intriguing.

'Come in, then,' Pecker invited.

Nervously Juttal stepped for the first time into a house as though he suspected some kind of trap. Nobby, satisfied the yard was in order, followed him to slump in his private corner. There were a lot of things to explore in that kitchen, all sorts of boxes, holes and corners, nooks and crannies and as he did so Pecker shaved at the sink, keeping half an eye on him through a piece of speckled mirror.

He could detect no animosity in either dog for the other, another obstacle climbed. Cheerfully he knotted the handkerchief at his throat: 'We can start leavin' the back door open again now, Nobby, y'can go out when yer like.' He pulled on his cap. 'I doubt they'd believe me in t'Spotted Dog but they'll see when y'go through them trials like a dose o' salts. An' no carryin' on while I'm out.' He went into the front room, slamming the door hard to engage the worn old latch.

The dogs spent the evening wandering in and out; once they had a game of chase that ended when they knocked the bucket over and it rolled clanking under the lean-to.

In a little more than a week Juttal was starting to accept as normal this environment that was totally foreign to him. If he had had a month it might be that he would have settled happily for the rest of his life.

Now he was a member of the household but a long way from joining the working team. Twice each day he went off the property to nearby fields for training sessions but when Pecker took Nobby to work in the day or night-time Juttal stayed at home. The back door was always left open to give him as much freedom as possible and he spent a lot of time lying in the doorway ready to run out at birds or if he saw a fieldmouse flitting amongst the tools or lumber.

Sometimes he would get a faint stirring of restlessness, an urge to be travelling the roads, seeing new places and revisiting the old ones. When he got one of these moods he would pace about the yard and round and round the kitchen, longing for the old free life. It was all right when Pecker and Nobby were there, the mock fights were fun and he was coming along with learning the exercises when the three of them went into the fields, he on the lead and educated Nobby working free.

The chance he was looking for came at the beginning of his third week.

Pecker had some trees to fell, which meant backing the van into the yard to load the tools and shutting Juttal up in the kitchen while the gates were open. For a change it was Juttal who got up in the window to watch Nobby out in the yard. The van backed in, stopped, Pecker got out and opened the rear doors, and felt for his cigarettes to find he had left them in the kitchen. Juttal was up at the window as he passed. Juttal was out in the yard, squeezing between Pecker's legs and the door casing before Pecker had time to grab him.

'Come, Dempsey! Come on, that's a good lad.'

Even as he tried he knew it was hopeless. As Juttal did not always obey the order when on the lead there was not the slightest chance of his doing so when off it.

Juttal ran to play with Nobby, or intended to at first, but he had not gone four yards when he saw the gates were standing open. Instantly Nobby and Pecker and the rudimentary lessons he was starting to obey were driven from his head. He skidded in a right-angled turn and ran through the gates into all the space he wanted. It was an accident that he turned right along the road, any direction was as good as another, until in the distance he saw the dark green wall of the escarpment and then his stride had purpose, he knew where he was going. If he heard Pecker's fading entreaties he showed no sign, going over the brow of a hill with the same sense of release as a child breaking up for the long summer holiday.

Standing in the middle of the road Pecker watched and shouted until he was out of sight, then he cursed himself for his stupidity in letting himself be caught off guard by a dog, the failing he sneered at in others. He knew there was no point in going after Juttal then, but he gussed and hoped Juttal would make his home in the cave again. 'Aye, Nobby, I've been a right berk. But we'll 'ave to get 'im back. Shouldn't be 'ard this time now 'e knows us.'

Juttal did not know of the attention he drew as he loped through the village of Sutton. Pecker had not made a secret of catching Juttal or the progress he was making in training him. Juttal had become rather a celebrity in the same way a reformed and truly repentant criminal might. The stories of his escapades and near captures were being retold and, of course, enlarged upon, and those who knew little about the ways of dogs—the big section of the public—were making the old mistake of endowing him with the thinking ability of a human. Now they would have it that he had outwitted Pecker by a devious and well-executed plan.

If Juttal had known of and understood his notoriety it is doubtful whether he would have cared. He stay with Pecker had not been traumatic or painful, in many ways it had been quite pleasant but it is as hard to anchor a born rover as it is to order the wind's direction.

Through the village on the winding road he came to the foot of the escarpment and increased his pace. As he left the road and galloped up the first slope he barked as a dog a quarter of his age might have done at the pure delight of living. Going north at a slanting angle across the face of the escarpment he burned some of the energy built up by his lazy way of living with Pecker, and when he got to the cave his whine of joy was a high squeal. Not many people would have believed that this romping playful animal was the savage brute they knew by hearsay.

Every inch of his territory had to be sniffed including the three tin cans Pecker had used as a warning bell, rusting now at the foot of the first slope down from the ledge. The ledge he would come back to sleep on in the afternoon before going to catch his dinner but until then there was some journeying to do and he went up over the drove-road with the moorland hills as his destination.

What would have been a journey of six miles to a bird was more like nine for Juttal, going by road or field, navigating by whim, through Cold Kirby and Old Byland and on across the River Rye to Rievaulx Moor to chase anything that moved.

Along the way his passage was noticed but no one attempted to apprehend him. From one ridge he stood looking down at a flock guarded by a man with two dogs whom he had seen before on his rounds and on some of the roads he crossed there were sheep left alone to crop the verges. All this, as everything was, was worth looking at but that was all, he had no desire to meddle in the affairs of others. But that was not apparent to people. The word went around that the wild dog was loose again, with the qualification that if Pecker Johnson could do nothing with him no one could, and he was a danger. A danger that must be removed for once and for all.

Alan Barnes heard about it from Archie Rowe who had been told by another farmhand passing the cattle grazing on his bicycle. They were eating the midday meal. Alan stabbed a cube of beef:

'So much for Pecker Johnson's bragging. Is it still hanging round Whitestone Cliff?'

'No, Sam Mills saw it goin' through Old Byland this mornin'.'

Alan grunted, 'It'll be most likely coming back here. I'll tell Mannie to start takin' the gun again.'

Alice Barnes said, 'Poor thing, it

won't know whether it's coming or going.'

'I do if it shows up on our land. It's going!'

'I tell yer,' Pecker Johnson said impatiently, 'I'd no chance o' stoppin' it an' there wa' no point in followin' it in the van just then, it wouldn't 'ave let me within 'undred yards. But don't worry, I'll 'ave it back. It's a bloody good 'un deep down, never 'ad a chance, that's all. While ever it sticks to rabbits no one's owt to worry about.'

Graham Maxwell was not as hopeful. 'It's all right saying that, *we* know it but you can't expect the farmers to take any chance of losing sheep.'

Pecker all but threw his cap to the ground, 'They make me bloody poorly, them farmers. The dog wa' loose for 'ow long? Did it offer t'touch a sheep—or a chicken or owt else? An' there's plenty o' rabbits, it won't go 'ungry.'

They were having a lunchtime pint with a sandwich in a small pub near the market place in Thirsk, having met by accident. Graham chewed thoughtfully,

226

'I can see your point. But Alan Barnes has one as well, you know, and it *is* wrong for a dog to be roaming in this country—anywhere at all, in fact.'

'I know, I know as well as you, but there's no need t'take the guns to it, it'll not do any 'arm...I'll tell yer, Graham, y'know I've 'ad some champion dogs an' I know what I'm talkin' about. Any dog'll train from a pup, a good handler'll 'appen make summat of a two-year-old, but older than that they're reckoned to have too many bad 'abits an' be past learnin'. That Lurcher's seven year old if 'e's a day an' I tell yer 'e was comin' on bloody smashin'. There's no need for 'im to be shot. Anyroad, wi' a bit of 'elp I'll 'ave 'im back tomorrer night. Leave 'im alone a day so's 'e'll feel safe an' it'll be easy.'

Graham drained his glass, 'As I said, you can count on me, and Jim McConnachie I should think, if the dog's still alive. Another pint?'

Pecker emptied his glass, 'Aye, go on then, an' I'll see yer in t'Spotted Dog tomorrer night.'

'You will.'

With the three dead trees on the outskirts of Thirsk felled Pecker was driving sedately homeward, eastbound on the A170. Up ahead, pulled off the road into a gateway was a police car. Pecker slowed and stopped athwart the Viva's bonnet and started to climb out. Johnnie put his head from the nearside window:

'Move on a bit, Pecker, you're in the way if we have to take off in a hurry.'

Pecker took off the handbrake and rolled a few yards down the hill. He strolled to the police car lighting a cigarette. He offered the packet to Johnnie who shook his head. 'We've both stopped, can't afford it on our pay.'

Pecker bent down to look through at Bill, 'What shift y'on, lads?'

'What's it look like? Days?'

Pecker nodded. 'Same tomorrer?'

'Aye.'

'Well,' Johnnie said to Bill, 'he's straightforward about it, asking us when it'll be safe to take his nets out.'

'And there's not many honest poachers knocking about, I'll tell you.'

'Give over,' Pecker grinned, 'if I tried to do owt bent you two Sherlock 'olmeses 'd'ave me.'

'We will one o' these days,' Bill promised him.

Johnnie looked at him cautiously. 'What y'askin' for, then?'

Pecker was still smiling, 'First I'll buy yer both a few pints to 'elp out wi' them poor wages, then I'll show yer summat about dog catchin.'

They, too, had heard the news and Johnnie grinned. 'Not that Lurcher again and anyway, imagine mouth-almighty-Pecker letting it escape.'

'An' y'know,' Pecker was unperturbed, 'that if it got away from me it'd get away from anyone.'

'Bloody hell! His head's still as big as Flamborough, Bill.'

'Bigger,' Bill laughed. 'Come on, Pecker, what's to do?'

'Well, when y're off duty yer can do as yer like, can't yer?'

'Within reason.'

Pecker grunted and explained to them what he had told Graham. In his enthusiasm he perhaps exaggerated Juttal's virtues but this only proved his sincerity.

Bill pulled a face, 'I don't know.'

'I'd be doin' nowt wrong,' Pecker pressed, 'You two've seen 'im, 'e's a grand dog.'

'He's a grand 'un all right, bitin' people.'

'Them that goes messin' about wi' dogs when they know nowt about 'em deserves to get bit. The dog wan't at fault wi' that schoolteacher. Come on, give 'im a chance.'

It was not too hard to persuade them to give up a couple of hours of leisure time. They were both animal lovers and Pecker left them with the promise that they could drink all the Old Peculiar they could force down—from twenty-past to half-past ten!

From there he went to see the vet and then up Sutton Bank to recruit Bernard Jackson, another softy where animals were concerned. With his team organised he went home, talking as usual to Nobby lying behind him in the back of the van.

Juttal carried on life at the cave where he had left it and for his first meal a fat pheasant provided itself, literally.

230

He was going south down the drove-road, making for the ledge in the late afternoon, when the bird whirred low over the road to land in the field on the escarpment side. The stone wall was low, Juttal cleared it with hardly a break in his acceleration, the great thighs and shoulders shooting him the ten yards to the bird before it could get off the ground again. It died instantly, a large cock bird, beautifully plumed, well-fleshed, one of nature's victims.

Juttal normally ate in the twilight because that was the time when rabbits were easiest to catch, but he had nothing against dining early and set to tearing out the annoying feathers as soon as he got home. The pheasant was fine, everything but the feathers, feet and head going down, and that afternoon's nap was blissful and dreamless.

The only thing was when he woke he was still a little peckish. A pheasant does not carry enough meat to satisfy a grown one-meal-a-day-dog, but that was easily put right. He went to get a rabbit. He made no mistakes, going to the burrow into the breeze, pounced and took a young buck. Really he needed only half a rabbit to supplement the pheasant, but like most dogs his creed was waste not want not and he made an effort to get the last shoulder into his crammed stomach. He managed it and practically crawled into the cave. It was well for him there was no attempt at recapturing him that night, bloated and lethargic he would have been easy prey for anyone.

Not sleepy, he lay with his head in the cave mouth watching the stars come out, listening to the night. A few clouds sailed over on the south-east wind, releasing a sudden clattering shower that wet his head, he hauled himself to the back of the cave knowing rain could mean thunder and as if trying to cut out the possibility he went to sleep.

The morning was damp and fresh, the air filled with the scents of all the greenery, the last drops of the last shower dripping from leaf to leaf to the rich earth, and the sun, two circumferences up from the horizon, was already pouring down enough warmth to make steam rise in the fields and woods.

The heat came late to the westerly

facing escarpment but Juttal could see the spreading country below was wide awake and living again. He came out of the cave to live with it.

He started that day as he would have liked to start all his days. He had a livening shake, made his toilet and trotted off directly north for a change along the face of the escarpment with all the other animals and birds making a respectful path for him. He saw many of them and did not mind their escaping, he was still too overloaded with food to bother making a game of chasing them.

He continued north, with wonderful panoramic views from the hill tops that he could not appreciate, past Hesketh Grange and Sneck Yate Bank, roughly following the Cleveland Way to Arden Great Moor 1200 ft above sea level. There his fancy turned him east where the wide, high moors, high crests and gills were all set at a downward tilt to the coast ending in a two-hundred-foot plunge into the North Sea.

Juttal knew nothing of visual beauty, to him objects were objects, some moving and some not, but breathtaking scenes are not everything. Juttal took great delight in being surrounded by unbounded space with the freedom to run far whenever and wherever he wanted and with a covetous eye in watching the wheeling gulls land—and chasing them back into the air where birds belonged. The land, everything wild in it and on it were Juttal's, Albert's legacy to him. In such a short time he had not forgotten Pecker or Nobby, they simply were not part of his life and so he did not think about them.

For Juttal the day was ideal. To him the blazing sunshine of the morning and the dull clouding of the afternoon were the same, just as the stiffening breeze was in the early evening when he lay, after sleeping, on the ledge waiting for hunting time. The wind had backed right around to the north-east and indicated rain which proved the pointer correct as he was finishing his dinner on the ledge.

It came down in long flashing lancets, the heavy grey drops, isolated at first, plunking into his coat, splashing on his nose. It was full dark before time that evening, the large warning drops increasing in density to a full-sized downpour and the low, thick clouds promising a prolonged dowsing.

From the blackness of the cave Juttal heard the rattling turn to a roar as the rain smashed through foliage, flattened the grass, and when, from far away, the wind carried the sound of rolling thunder he turned his face to the back of the cave, covering his nose with his tail. Next time the thunder was closer, a distinct crack, and he stiffened and whimpered.

It was cosy enough in the Spotted Dog taproom as the rain had started too late to keep anyone at home and the drumming on the window was covered by a dozen loud conversations and orders shouted at the barman.

Commandeering one table were Pecker, the two policemen, Bernard Jackson, the vet and the Inspector of the RSPCA. None of them was pleased about the rain, none except Pecker who grinningly said it would make it even easier for him to get his dog back.

'We'll be on top on 'im afore 'e 'ears us comin'.'          235 _min'.'

His volunteer force made various derisory comments, Bill saying to Johnnie, 'We must be bloody daft, we could be going home to bed with the wife.'

'Never mind, it'll onny tek 'alf an hour or so,' Pecker consoled him.

They were cheered a little when one latecomer announced from the doorway as he shook his cap that the rain was easing and the sky breaking up, and when they went out to the cars at a quarter to eleven it had stopped and the wind was dropping.

They went in three vehicles to park at the bend in the road at the bottom of the escarpment. Jim McConnachie went with Graham Maxwell, the two policemen in Johnnie's second-hand Ford, Bernard Jackson with Pecker, and when they got out Pecker led the way up the farm road to a point directly under Juttal's cave. They did not talk, Pecker had told them what he wanted over the beer, and they put their rubber-booted feet down carefully. Leaving the road they walked silently in file up through the trees to gather at the foot of the second slope down from the cave, Pecker directing them with hand signals. They spread out and started to climb, the going slippy and precarious on the wet grass, and before they reached the narrow plateau it was thundering again in the south. The rain was coming back.

Juttal had been unable to sleep at all with the bangs in the sky, the flickering lightning, the wind moaning and rattling branches. He had lain and shivered but not from cold.

The thunder had gone away, the rain had stopped, the noise of the wind had decreased and still he could not sleep. He had on him one of the moods of restlessness that were getting stronger as the spring wore on. At this time of the year he should not be on the escarpment, he should be to the south guarding the caravan against the other gipsy dogs at one of the fairs, he knew that, but it needed a very strong pull to take him away from his present idyllic way of living. Whatever his thoughts—if he had thoughts as such—were on, that subject were interrupted when he heard the thunder coming back and shortly after that the sound of slithering and scrambling somewhere below the cave. Not even the threat of being exposed to thunder and lightning held him in the cave then.

He went out on to the ledge and saw them at once as they gained the plateau, a party of men who as they began to climb his slope could only be coming to one place. His head lowered, lips lifted and he snarled the warning that he was ready to fight for what was his. One of the men in the middle of the line looked up:

'Nah then, Dempsey lad, I've come t' take yer 'ome.'

For an instant Juttal stopped growling, Pecker was not like other men, he had for a time been the master and a good one even though he had kept Juttal shut up in the yard. He had given Juttal good food, things he had never tasted before, and if Pecker had been alone he might have been allowed to go right up to the cave. But he was not alone and the other men with him had to be stopped. Juttal snarled his protracted warning

238

again but still the men toiled up the slope with Pecker all the time talking soothingly.

As they climbed the line shortened, they were converging on the cave, a form of attack new to Juttal. One man he would have flown at for stepping over the boundary but if he went for one there would be the others to take possession of the cave. Uncertain he ran backward and forward along the ledge, snarling and barking at them all until the nearest of them, Pecker, was only two yards away and now Juttal could see he was carrying the muzzle and lead. The men on either side of Pecker had nooses and Juttal barked at the equipment as much as at the men.

The men stopped at the distance of two yards, Pecker said something and came on alone with his friendly talk and stifling muzzle. The poacher had been quite right in guessing Juttal would not attack him but at the same time Juttal had no intention of letting him put the contraption over his head. There were two alternatives, attack or run. As attacking Pecker was out of the question he

239

allowed himself to be driven from his home, running to Pecker's right off the ledge, down the slope, easily evading Johnnie's outstretched arms and Bill's desperate dive, hearing Pecker yell, 'Grab 'im!'

Juttal went on through the trees to the north, running a long way from the dangers at the cave until he was too tired to go any further, the intermittent thunder helping to drive him, and when he curled up under the trailing branches of a willow he slept through all but the loudest overhead rendings.

# CHAPTER 8

Juttal had spent the night not far from Kepwick Bank, some five miles to the north of the cave, and his home to the south was the first thing to come into his head when the birds woke him up.

He came out from under the willow to a blustery day that offered little promise to holidaymakers and to which Juttal was indifferent. His first inclination was to go home but with the picture of his ledge with the hole at the rear came also the picture of men waiting, men who would not leave him alone, men with nets and nooses and leads and collars and enclosed yards to lock him in. Another dog, unable to fend for itself, would perhaps have welcomed the men but Juttal with his self-sufficiency was becoming, if not afraid, certainly timorous of man. So he did not go to the cave, he went eastward with the gusting wind tossing his coat, to parts where no one had ever tried to catch him, the high moors.

In that country it is impossible to travel very far in a straight line, the roads twist, turn, climb and plunge, narrow metalled ribbons for the convenience of men which Juttal could take or leave. On that journey, taking the easiest line all the time he crossed the roads, using the heather and fern tracts, thickly-wooded hillsides and on the lower slopes the enclosed fields to make his aimless way.

Aimless but not hapless. An observer would have said he looked as though he knew exactly where he was going with his steady trot on the level ground, the swinging lope down the hills and the powerful thrusting bounds when climbing. Almost every time he came over a wall to cross a road he caused small hearts to beat with fear, feeding rabbits and partridges each taking flight in their own way, but he was not hungry at that hour and there would be plenty of rabbits and partridges when he was.

He crossed Hawnby Moor without finding anything worth his time, dropped down into Bilsdale and forded the narrow River Seph, climbing again to East Moors.

On East Moors there was an old ruined building, a heap of derelict masonry he used as a hostel for a couple of hours' sleep out of the wind and then he moved due south on the third leg of a square. He stayed on the high ridge connecting East Moors with Rievaulx Moor, the thousand-foot hump with the spruce forest covering its east slope and the west side running down into Laskhill Pasture and the valley with the wriggling Seph. South-east he trotted for more than a mile, to where the cushiony heather-covered ground ended and he was looking down over the spikey tops of the evergreen trees into the Rye Valley, the mass of High Banniscue heaving out of the fork where the Seph joins the Rye.

He had unconsciously been heading for home on the escarpment but he now had every cause to fear for his safety in that place. Up here deep in the hills he could pick out the homes of the hill farmers and houses meant men, but at that moment there was not one human in sight, just the distant cattle in the valley and the sheep on the slopes and the area bristling with game.

He went over the edge to scramble down through the close-growing trees —one of the many parts of the widely-scattered Rievaulx Forest—and he found another home under a cut-back bank. Not a cave, not as snug and cosy and weatherproof, amply sheltered though for the worst of summer weather. He was a long time sniffing about his new territory, acclimatising himself and examining the bottom of the nearby trees until he was satisfied and took possession by curling up under the bank and at once he felt at home.

Food was no more of a problem, either. On his first sunset hunt he climbed back up to the moor, surprised a hare and caught it in one hundred and fifty yards, a fine specimen that was too much for one meal, really, but all he left was the head, paws, and a few bones to mark where he lived. He had another four days of what were to him perfect living. As regularly as any office worker he left home to go about his business of exploring, to the north-east into the very heart of some of the wildest terrain in the country which makes up the National Park. He roamed and ranged as far as Glaisdale Moor at the head of Great Fryup Dale with its little tributary of the Esk, in those five days learning more about the geography than a man on foot would have done in a month. Juttal's built-in compass, his pinpoint sense of direction was as great an asset as his speed, strength and stamina.

He had no special place for hunting as he had had on the escarpment. He noted at once that the best hunting grounds for him were the roads, to which in the mornings and evenings the rabbits and partridges seemed to be drawn by a magnet. A dog without his hunting ability would not have gone hungry, sometimes there was a dead rabbit every two or three hundred yards, killed accidentally by vehicles, some a little mangled and some flattened beyond recognition but still food for a needy dog.

On the fourth evening he came down off Shaw Ridge, stealthily, on the heather cushion, shielded by the ferns to the narrow road in Ouse Gill. By chance he used the eastern slope as soon as he saw the road below and the heights of Shaw Ridge threw a concealing shadow to help him. He knew from his days with Albert that a partridge will take to the air when startled, but often it will run a few yards first and Juttal had the duration of this ungainly sprint to make his catch and kill.

The dry stone wall was low and on his way down he saw several of the brown birds moving about in the grass of the roadside verge, several rabbits bob-hopping backwards and forwards across the road. He could not see over the wall when he came within six feet of it and that was where the element of luck entered hunting. With two strides he went up and over, his feet lightly touching the top of the wall as he leapt in amongst them. He used the purchase of the wall top to change direction right to where a group of three partridges were searching the grass. They scattered and Juttal, single-minded, went for the one in the middle which ran directly away from him. He caught it in the air, making a final jump and getting his teeth into the short tail feathers, a quick flurry, a scattering of feathers and it was over. With the partridge hanging from his mouth he scaled the wall again and went, in as straight a line as the hills permitted, south-west for home.

The little triumph or tragedy, depending on the point of view, had not gone unwitnessed. Pecker Johnson was not the only poacher who made at least part of his living on the moors. Perhaps he was the only one to regard poaching, proudly, as his profession, but there were others who came for sport as much as the pot, rabbit specialists with ferrets and nets and those who fancied themselves as crack shots and liked the taste of game bird flesh.

One such man, George Hepworth, was a city dweller—an iron moulder by trade—whose primary pleasure was to take his rod to forbidden waters or his .22 air rifle anywhere where there were desirable targets. George considered himself a sportsman and his idea of hunting was not to use beaters and shotguns—possibly because he would never have the means—but to stalk within thirty or forty yards and kill cleanly with a single slug. He had paid eighty pounds for his gun, an excellent accurate weapon made in Germany, a Model 50, and with it he had proved that the manufacturers were playing safe with the range. George had killed more than one running rabbit stone dead at fifty to fifty-five yards.

When Juttal had come over the wall George had been coming quietly from the opposite direction on the other side of the road, crouched behind the wall and taking a furtive look every few yards. He was sixty yards away when Juttal made his speedy advance and retreat and if curses had been shotgun pellets there would have been a very dead dog on the roadside.

In some respects George's sense of morality was the same as the late Albert's. Within his own code he would not steal. He believed himself to be an honest man and would have argued the poaching laws with the Lord Chief Justice. Where he differed from the gipsy was in his conviction that all the game running in any of his favourite places belonged to him; his moralities were rather contradictory.

He had heard talk in the country pubs about the wily wild dog and knew from the description who had robbed him. Not only robbed him of the fat partridge but ruined his chance of taking anything else. In a very black humour he turned about to walk back to his car. There was about an hour of light left, time to try somewhere else. He could get back to the car in twenty minutes and a fast drive on the little-used roads would get him to another favourite place, Bonfield Gill to the south-west.

Juttal had gone perhaps half a mile, had splashed across Hodge Beck and was climbing up to Packley Moor when nature gave him a present. On the heather-covered hillside he was amongst a colony of feeding rabbits before he or they realised it. In the first surprised moment he dropped his partridge to go after a leaping buck and the rabbit's speed was cut down by the profuse heather and fern. Juttal got it in fifty yards, a snapping shake of the head and he went back to the partridge. He dropped the rabbit to pick up the bird, paused, dropped the bird to pick up the rabbit. He did this repeatedly finding that whichever he chose the other was always on the ground and not in his mouth. The custom of eating at home was strong in him, that was what he wanted to do. It finally occurred to him to pick up both at the same time and he pushed them about on the heather until he became short-tempered that his mouth was not big enough. The only solution was some time in coming to him. He would eat one now and take the other home. He set about the partridge, making short work now that he was a fairly skilful poultry dresser, and as even a big partridge was not a full meal for him, with his appetite whetted he ate the rabbit there as well. And then he was overloaded. But happy. He picked up his course again over Packley Moor and down into Bonfield Gill.

The old 3 litre Rover hummed down from the north into Bonfield Gill, singing along the straights, swooping round bends, into dips and over crests. Reckless driving for the narrow road but George Hepworth knew how little the road was used. Tourists found it by accident and the farms were scattered and few. Furthermore his car was in perfect mechanical order and could, he boasted, stop on a teacake.

Every quarter mile or so the verge had been levelled and scooped back from the road to give vehicles passage room. In one of these miniature laybys George left the car, took the air rifle from the back seat and vaulted the wall. In a dip three hundred yards ahead he was sure there would be a target and he was hoping for a bird, pheasant or partridge or pigeon. But rabbit would do. Poached meat, like stolen apples, tasted better but it was the stalking, his marksmanship and the thrill of breaking a law he did not recognise which gave him most pleasure.

In a crouching run he moved a hundred yards, stopped for a peep over the wall, bent forward and ran on. When he got to where the road dipped he raised his head very slowly and through a notch in the dry stones saw what he wanted to see, two partridges on the far verge about seventy yards away. At the halfway distance to the birds a stone jutted out from the wall, a convenient marker, and if he could not score a killing hit at thirty-five yards he would throw his gun away. And in the fading light he knew that would still rate as a fine shot.

Doubling again he slowed his pace, placing his feet very carefully. At the marker he raised his head again to see both birds had moved on three or four yards, feeding away from him. He had eyes for nothing but the birds and if the landowner had appeared George would still have got in his shot. The ease with which the butt came to his shoulder told of long practice, the sights lined effortlessly with the trailing bird's head and his finger began to squeeze. For an instant the bird stopped foraging to raise its head and George had perfect alignment on the two-cell brain when Juttal came over the wall almost on top of it. The partridges called out in fear and warning, breaking into the take-off sprint and George watched in disbelief at the same thing happening to him twice in the same hour in two different places. Juttal was only crossing the road but George did not know that. If he had paused he could have watched the dog leap the second wall and disappear toward Bogmire Gill. But George Hepworth did not pause. Knowing next to nothing about the simple process of canine thinking he tried to teach him the folly of disturbing humans at their sport. He swung the gun from the space where the partridge's head had been, aimed and triggered off a shot at Juttal's hind quarters which were outlined for a fraction of a second on top of the wall. The hard cough of the rifle, the slap of lead meeting living flesh and Juttal's howl of pain were nearly simultaneous, the pellet driving deep to the thigh bone.

Ammunition of that size has neither the velocity or weight to knock an animal of Juttal's size over; it was the raking pain, landing on a numbing leg that caused him to fall in a sideways tumbling roll.

'That'll learn yer,' George Hepworth shouted, brandishing the the Model 50. He did not wait to see what happened to Juttal. Disgusted and angry he went back

253

to his car with nothing in the bag and the light too far gone for there to be any hope that day.

When Juttal scrambled to his feet the sharp burn of the pain was dulling, bearable as long as he kept his right hind paw off the ground but when it did touch it was excruciating, like being shot again. He did not know he had been shot, he did not wonder what caused the agony, he only knew it had suddenly come, that it was difficult and nigh impossible to climb these hills without using all four legs, although he tried to persevere on his original course.

George Hepworth's act of vexation was to make yet another change in the life of Juttal.

From Bonfield Gill to Rievaulx Moor was a climb through the conifers of 400 ft and then there was a two mile trek across the rough moorland to his home in the trees on the other side. The climb he could take easily at the lope defeated him before he was a quarter of the way up, the strain of trying to take all his weight on his forelegs as he kept his wounded leg clear of the ground tore at his shoulder muscles and he let himself fall over sideways under the low branches of a young spruce. He yelped softly as he jarred his nagging hip. Then, with true fatalism, he lay there panting because there was nothing else he could do. Except lick away the occasionally trickling blood and watch the last of the daylight go, the trees and hills turn from green to grey to black.

There were, of course, all the noises to listen to as near and far the nightly dramas went on, the stalking, the chasing, the pouncing, the narrow escapes, the quick killings as every living creature fought in its own way to survive until the sun came up again. And of all the wild creatures eking out a living in the meadows and moors and woods Juttal would have been king if only men had left him alone.

The stars were high on that moonless night, giving only enough light to separate the sky from the black earth, a night when the sense of smell was paramount for attack or defence. As Juttal dropped off to sleep the breeze was bringing him the scent of many furtive fellow creatures.

He woke some time in the smallest hours, instantly picking up the giveaway pungent odour of a dog fox. The fox, upwind, had not detected Juttal and was coming up the hill at a run, carrying a young rabbit back to the den. When Juttal could see the glisten of the almond eyes he snarled just once. The fox paused for the shortest instant, broke to the left and was gone into the trees. Juttal put his head back on his paws and slept again.

When he woke the stirring woods were echoing the low morning crescendo of clacking and clicking, cheeping, whirring and trilling. An overhead rustle plunked heavy dewdrops into the damp grass when a marten sped after a flashing squirrel.

Juttal swallowed on his hot thirst and, forgetting his wound, tried to spring to his feet. He yelped as much with surprise as pain and staggered into the tree trunk, trying to keep his right hind paw off the ground. He shivered, had another painful swallow and set off down the hill. He must have water and the nearest was the stream coming out of Bonfield Gill.

It was a slow business going down through the trees, each step a considered effort, and it took a long time. And then there was the road with its two walls to cross, walls he had taken in his stride yesterday, walls that now looked insurmountable—almost. Not quite because he *had* to scale them, he *had* to have water.

He knew that farther to the north the road crossed the water. If he went that way he would not have to climb the walls but standing between was a farm, he could see smoke coming from the chimney in the distance, and at the farm would be men whom he did not want to see. Juttal never wanted to see any men again with their nets and nooses and kennels and restrictions.

At this point the walls were no more than three feet high, the rough stones giving plenty of purchase, and when his one-legged leap failed and his chest hit the wall top he scrabbled with his good hind leg and jerked with his body until he rolled over. It hurt when he hit the grass verge, it hurt when he limped across the road and scrambled over the second wall, it hurt all the hobbling way to the stream, but when he dipped his muzzle in the clean, cold, trickling water it was worth it. With his tongue working like a piston he lapped and lapped, paused when he had washed away the burning dryness, the went on to drink his fill.

Then he had to get home. All the way up through the woods again, the two miles across the moor and down the other side. A human would have quailed at the thought with a throbbing hip and useless leg but Juttal could not think in front or imagine the hardship of the journey so he set off, meeting each obstacle as it came up. A trip that would normally have taken him half an hour at most took him five hours of starting, stopping and resting, struggling up again to limp on. Climbing the walls was most sharply painful but over and done with quickly, the laborious drag up to the moorland plateau seemed interminable, an unending nagging ache with the ridge never getting any closer. When he finally pulled himself on to the heather cushion he had to lie down to rest overworked muscles, to regain his breath, to wait for the throbbing to stop.

Crossing the moor was a different problem, the stiff matted heather snatching at his feet, trying to pull him down. He stopped many times, more and more frequently as the fatigue set into his bones and joints and when at last he collapsed into his sleeping place the sun was at the top of its arc.

He was thirsty again, terribly thirsty and the nearest water now was far down and across the road, the silvery River Rye. By raising his head he could see the swift water gleaming in the sunlight, tempting, tantalizing as it slid through the trees and bushes but he had not the strength to get down there. After the terrific effort of getting home all he could do was lie and shiver from his fever.

He unwittingly indulged in the best medicine for a wild animal; sleep. His heavy weariness drew him down into a deep unconsciousness, a sleep so deep and long that the passing of a herd of horses would hardly have disturbed him. It can be dangerous for a wild and

259

hunted animal to have all its senses dulled at once and anyone could have walked up to put a dog-catcher over his head, but no one did and when he awoke the complete rest had done him good. The fever had subsided, the pain of the wound dulled to an inconvenient stiffness which gave him a slight twinge when he moved.

It was very dark with thick cloud hiding the stars but all he had to do was keep on going down until he got to the water. The descent took a long time, particularly the last steep drop from the road to the river and he did not hurry about his drinking, he drank twice with a good rest in between before starting back. When he got back home after a lot of stopping he had asked too much of his body; he was bone weary and fell again into that heavy slumber, completely dead to the world. And the next time he woke he was hungry.

He did not go out to find something to eat, it was too late in the day, mid morning, dawn and dusk were the hunting times and he was not so ravenous that he could not wait. And it was very pleasant to lie drowsing, there was no discomfort at all as long as he kept still, and in any case he could hear the cars buzzing up and down the road. Cars meant men. To the north above the river fork he could see across the Seph a flock being driven up High Bannescue by a shepherd with two dogs, a cluster of white dots as they toiled upward. The shepherd left them at the top to feed their way down and at that moment, to Juttal, the sheep were just something to watch with detached interest.

It was a long wait, unable to make his daily journey, simply letting the time pass until the hunting hour. Sometimes he saw men, always at a distance with sheep or cattle or on the broad service tracks cutting through the heavily-timbered slope across the Rye valley. Once a caravan was towed off the road into the old quarry directly below Juttal and the people got out of the car to light a primus stove and make a meal. Distant though they were Juttal could see them eating and his mouth filled and overflowed with saliva but he would not have gone down to them if they had been offering him food. When they drove away the sun was far down, the world was quietening, becoming peaceful. It was the time to hunt.

It was now two days since he had eaten, his contracted stomach not exactly painful but more of a sharp spur to his senses as he three-legged his way up to the moor. He was generally stiff but apart from his damaged leg the rest of his body responded, loosening up with exercise.

He had chosen the moor as that was where he would most likely pick up a hare and a hare would give him the biggest meal of the animals he looked on as legal prey. Not that he would spurn a rabbit or pheasant if he came across one but it was with the desire for a big meaty hare that he came up from the trees on to the open land.

He came stealthily on to the heather, slowly, with the breeze coming into his face as it should be and at once picked out four feeding rabbits. They were twenty yards away, noses into the wind, and he would cover half the distance before they heard him and took flight, before they were in full stride he would make up the remaining ten yards and take the slowest of them. That was how it always was. Rabbits were easy to catch.

But that was not how it came out this time. He had only covered a quarter of the way when they heard him and when they leapt off he might have been standing still, they outran him so easily. He did not give up. He followed until the back marker had disappeared into the ground but all the time they had been gaining on him.

He limped on eastward, into the wind, accidentally flushing a hare. With a bare five yards start the hare should have been no problem, should have been hanging from Juttal's mouth in twenty or thirty yards, but it was the same again and if the rabbits had left him as though he were standing the hare vanished so quickly that Juttal might have been moving backwards.

He persevered with the hunt and caught nothing on the moor. When it was too dark he went back past his home down to the road looking for birds but they had all gone to roost. He knew the rabbits often ran about in the quarry so he tried his luck there to be disappointed again.

But he did find something. Amongst the litter left by inconsiderate picnickers was some skin and the leg bones of a chicken and he was so hungry he ate them there and then. There was not nearly enough to fill him, only enough to whet his appetite, but there was nothing else and, tired out again, he made the slow climb back to the overhang.

It was a time of great misfortune for Juttal, he was living through one of those chains of unlucky events which often dictate the way a life will go from that point onwards.

When he went to sleep that night it was to the sigh of the breeze through the tree tops but long before the dawn the breeze died, the air turned sultry and farm-house barometers dropped dramatically through RAIN TO STORM. And storm it did.

In a dim greyness that should have been bright daylight jagged blue lightning ripped across the sky, the frightening thunder followed in a cracking, booming roll and the trees and moors were pounded with a heavy vertical downpour. Juttal trembled, tried to draw deeper into the shallow overhang, but his wounded leg stuck stiffly out and was drenched in seconds. He closed his eyes and whimpered.

An early primitive might have been forgiven for thinking the heavens had gone mad. Sometimes far away and too often overhead the lightning danced its quick haphazard path with the thunder bellowing in its wake, drowning the drumming of the rain, the splashing of the new cascades pouring down the hillside. A sheet of water hit Juttal's leg, then another and then his overhang became a waterfall, drenching him, chilling him, but he dared not go out into the open under the thunder.

The initial torrent slackened and at noon the rain stopped but the sky was still dark, the atmosphere oppressively threatening the miserable wet world. All afternoon the lightning flashed intermittently as the water drained away down to the swollen river, and at what should have been sunset it all started again.

With a blazing blue-white flash that lit

up the world for seconds on end and a prolonged explosive roar which vibrated the heavy air, the monsoon-like rain smashed down again making a hissing rumble as it battered the foliage. In the worst electric storm in living memory Juttal lay whimpering, whining, terrified, petrified, oblivious that he was lying inside a cataract when the water poured again from the overhang, conscious only of the noise he hated.

It was more than seventy-two hours since his last meal discounting the picnic scraps and his stomach had shrunk to a griping constant pain, but he would not have moved three feet from his inadequate shelter for the biggest meal of his life.

The storm was neither short nor sharp, doing widespread damage to the crops down on the plain, washing away bridges, flooding the lower pastures, turning runnels into streams, streams into rivers, ponds into lakes.

The fury lasted in full force until after midnight and then abated so gradually that it was an hour before Juttal noticed any change. By three o'clock the rain had stopped and with it the lightning, but the massive excess water still rolled down the hillside, gushed noisily over Juttal's home and was still draining away when, as if Nature had decided to show how abandoned it could be, the wind began to rise. Blowing from the east it swayed the trees, showering down the collected water until it was as if the rain had come back.

The shrieking gale dispersed the clouds so that when the sun rose the day was as light as it should be, but Juttal had to stay where he was, not daring to go out in what built up to be a hurricane. He heard, more than once, the dreadful tearing as the wind killed a tree and many times, over the insane howling, the snap and crash of falling branches. For seven hours the angry wind ripped at the North Country doing damage amounting to millions of pounds in town, city and country, and nowhere in it all was there a more fearful heart than Juttal's.

In the middle of the forenoon the wind force decreased perceptibly and by early afternoon could be classed as no stronger than a moderate breeze. The water had stopped coming down from the overhang and with a bright sun there was the promise of one of the unpredictable changes in the weather that are part of the British climate.

Juttal came out into the open, drenched and mud splattered. One happy side effect of the storm was that his leg was much easier. It was still fairly stiff but the pain was bearable when he unthinkingly put the paw to the ground. He also managed a limited shake, something he had not been able to enjoy, and then he went hunting. It was not the proper time of day but convention goes by the board when the stomach has been shrinking for nearly four days. His need for food was critical to replace the strength lost by the combined effect of being shot and then starved and he went up the hillside to the moor with the power of desperation.

His eagerness to sink his teeth into meat was partly his undoing, that and his impaired speed. Instead of coming up on to the plateau carefully, slowly, he burst over the edge, eyes sweeping, nose working. The first he saw of the rabbits was their bobbing scuts as they ran for safety and when he went after them he did not even lessen the gap let alone gain ground. Considering he had what was still a rather heavy limp he was very fast, but at three-quarter speed he had no chance of making a kill.

He carried on trying, running at anything that moved including the gulls and he did not have what could have been called a near miss, everything got into the air or under the ground whilst he was still yards away.

That afternoon Juttal tried everything he knew, outrunning or stalking were equally unsuccessful, getting him only another raging thirst. He did not have to go to the river, there were plenty of rainwater pools left in the gullies and hollows and he was lapping at a puddle at the base of a tree when he heard the lamb calling, the plaintive repeated bleat of a lost sheep. He heard the whistle of a shepherd and made his way back up to the moor, away from the man.

The promised change of weather had materialised and the sunset was a calm warm red-gold indication of a fair tomorrow, for that part of the country an appropriate shepherd's delight. To Juttal it was the end of his most frustrating day, weary again, starved to the point of madness. His last three attempts to catch rabbits had been ludicrous. He stood head down on the edge of the moor, utterly dejected, defeated, when for the second time that evening he heard the cry of a lost lamb.

It was coming from his left, somewhere not far down the hillside in the trees and the sound drew him. He limped quickly along the rim until he was above the bleating and in the beautiful gold-tinged evening light he saw it thirty yards down the slope. There was no flock nearby, no high whistle to tell of a man, the lamb must have wandered a long way, and for a long time, until the white shape was a pale blur under the trees, Juttal watched it and saw it only as life saving food. Forbidden food, food he had never up to that point even contemplated taking. But now, unable to catch the food he had been taught to take, he was driven into going against the rules by which his life had been regulated.

He went down the darkening slope to put himself forever outside the law, to lower himself to the same level as the fox and make himself a legitimate target for the gun of any man. In the closing darkness a bleat of alarm came up from the trees and during the short scuffle a high-pitched cry of terror. And then the rustling movements could have been those of any animal in the undergrowth.

# CHAPTER 9

It had been pointless trying to sleep through it, the drumming rain had been bad enough but ranked as a whisper compared with the tearing wind. At half-past four he had gone down to the kitchen to find his mother already there with the fire crackling and the kettle boiling.

'I thought you'd be up,' he yawned. 'What a bloody night!' Alice Barnes was afflicted with the common fear of thunder and lightning and refused to stay above ground level, if the farm had boasted a cellar she would have been below ground. She tried to hide her nervousness but her voice was scratchy. 'This is the worst I've ever known, I wish it'd stop.'

'It's only the wind, now, it'll soon blow itself out. Go back to bed.'

She shook her head and poured boiling

water into the teapot. 'I couldn't sleep through this lot any more than you.'

In the solid old farmhouse they had to speak louder than normal over the devil's symphony. With the constant roar was a high-pitched fluting as a taut wire acted as a woodwind reed, a loosened piece of board flapped and boomed on the side of the barn, the house windows rattled and from somewhere came a tortured creaking. Periodically a downdraught drove the smoke back down the chimney, spreading a black cloud along the ceiling.

Alan did his best to cheer her up with light talk that was pitifully and obviously forced and when he heard a mighty snap and crash as something gave way to the wind he sat silent, drinking his tea, trying to stop visualising the devastation that must be out there. He could, if it had not been for his mother, have packed his bags there and then and left Lane End forever with the first light, letting the bank salvage what it could from the wreckage and to hell with everyone and everything, but he did have his mother to think of so it was out of the question.

Suddenly the kitchen window caved in,

showering the sink unit with glass fragments and something bounced across the roof with a succession of thuds. Protruding into the room through the window was the ragged end of a broken branch three inches in diameter and if Alice had been at the sink at the wrong moment she could have been killed. As it was she was stunned, saying:

'God, when's it going to stop?'

That was when Archie came running down, boots unfastened, buttoning his trousers, 'Summat's smashed t'roof in over my head. House'll be in bits if this keeps up.' He helped Alan to push the branch clear of the window frame and partly block the hole with an overturned coffee table from the sitting-room.

Having done the best they could they could only sit and wait it out and listen as the havoc went on. At eleven o'clock the wind had dropped enough for them to go out with reasonable safety and the three of them stood silently in the middle of the yard. There was nothing to say. One half of the wooden roof of the byre had been blown away, apparently rolling on end across the house roof and breaking the slates in two places, giving the wind the purchase needed to snatch away the rest of the slates on that side of the apex. With the laths and beams showing, the window broken, the house looked derelict. What had been an orderly farmyard was now a dump of debris, broken slates and tree branches, wheel-barrows, tubs and drums overturned, the chicken house leaning perilously, the snapped telephone cable flying like a pennant of doom in the wind. Alan stared at the roofless byre, shook his head and walked slowly back into the house, Archie touched Alice's shoulder. 'You go see to him, I'll 'ave a look at the cattle.'

Alice pulled back her shoulders and nodded. This final—surely it must be final—setback was by far the worst suffered at Lane End. From now on things must surely improve but the damage would not repair itself. There was long days of toil ahead and she would have to snap her son out of his understandable despondency, convince him that, as he had said with such hope in the beginning, it would come out all

275

right in the end.

But defeated as he felt he needed no urging to start putting things to rights and after a good breakfast took the tractor and trailer to the builder's merchants in Kirby-moorside while Archie started clearing up the yard. On the way he called to see the Fairbrothers whose cottage, on the leeside of the high hill, had escaped without a scratch. One section of the fence around the sheep pen had been blown down and a few sheep had got out but the dogs would soon find them.

That evening when the sun was going down in its glorious blaze Alan Barnes was recovering, was more like himself. The yard had been put back in good order, the chicken house levelled up, the kitchen window securely boarded while awaiting delivery of a new frame, and a quarter of the slates were back on the roof. Of all the terrible widespread damage Lane End Farm had been hardest hit in that area and Pecker Johnson had made it number one priority, with Alan and Archie serving as his labourers.

Pecker was last down the ladder and

he moved to the corner of the house for a clear view of the dipping sun. 'No chance of any rain ternight, y'll be safe enough while we get it finished termorrer.'

Archie grinned. 'That's Lane End luck, mate, it never rains 'ere when the roof gets blown off.'

Even Alan had to smile at his irrepressible cowman, 'Come on in, dinner'll be ready.

Alice was putting the meal out as they trudged in. For once the garrulous Archie was too ravenous to deliver his monologue and the food went down quickly and silently.

Although Pecker's own style of cooking suited him he did like a meal prepared by an expert whenever the chance came along. Without a word he pushed away his cleaned dinner plate and replaced it with a dish of strawberry pie topped with a snowball of clotted cream. his spoon and jaws worked methodically, oblivious of Alice's amused observation. When his dessert dish was as bare as his dinner plate he looked up for the first time and opened his mouth but Alice beat him to it. She already had another wedge of pie balancing on a cake knife, slid it on to his dish and with her left hand delivered a dollop of cream. He grunted and turned his eyes down.

The hunger that had stopped Archie from talking had not stopped him watching points and as he accepted a second helping he grinned:

'Y'd think Pecker'd 'ad nowt to eat since Christmas. Time yer got married, Pecker lad, a good woman'd fatten y'up.'

'What about you?' Pecker retorted between shovelling spoonfuls.

Archie grinned wider, 'I've got one to look after me, I've no need to get married.'

'Yes,' Alice mused slowly, 'I think we'll have to get you fixed up with a little woman, Pecker, it's not tood for a man to live on his own. Who do we know, Alan?'

Alan did not much want to join in meaningless chit-chat but the heavy meal made him more relaxed and he contributed thoughtfully, 'There's Molly Gough down in Thirlby and she's a woman who *can* cook. Y'd be laughin' there, Pecker. I think she fancies you, an' all.'

'Yes, Molly's just right,' Alice beamed as if perfectly serious. 'A nice little cottage thrown in as well. Pity the line's down, I'd ring her up and get her to go for a drink with you tonight.' Pecker could only snort his derision but Archie leered. 'Think of 'er all terrified an' no one to cuddle up to in that storm, all on 'er own an' prayin' for someone like you to protect her.'

'Get st—' Pecker held the profanity back just in time. He grinned. 'Sorry, Alice, but anyroad I've summat else on me mind just now I'm tryin' to pinpoint where Dempsey's 'olin' up.'

'Dempsey?' Alice queried.

'That Lurcher I let get away.'

Archie slurped at his tea, 'Still set on gettin' it back?'

'Aye. I will, an' all.'

The mention of Juttal brought back to Alan one of his imagined causes for his long spell of bad luck and the better humour they had been working him into dropped away again. He glowered, 'I've told you what I'll do if I see the bloody thing first. The gun's still in the car.'

Pecker knew that to defend the dog would be a waste of time and when Archie asked where he thought the dog was living he shrugged negatively. He actually had a very good idea, he had made a careful note of recently reported sightings and all were centred around Rievaulx Moor. With his wide knowledge of dogs, and working on the basis that Juttal was fundamentally as much a creature of habit as the rest of his kind, he deduced the stray would look for the same type of home he had adopted on the escarpment, some kind of fairly inaccessible cave that would be easy to defend. There were dozens of places fitting that description on the wooded slopes surrounding Rievaulx Moor but with patience, Nobby's keen nose and powerful pair of binoculars, Pecker was perfectly sure he would recapture the dog he looked upon as a challenge to his ability.

Pecker lit a cigarette and looked at Alan. 'Y'know, yer've got that dog wrong, it's not a bad 'un it's a bloody good 'un an' I'll prove it when I get 'im back agen. I know you think 'e put the wind up your sheep but I'll bet me 'ouse an' land 'e didn't. That old gipsy brought 'im up right.'

'I can see you believin' that seein' as it knows how to pinch game.' Alan's returning bitterness was in the insult and Alice quickly changed the subject back to the safe one of pretending to match-make for Pecker.

Mannie Fairbrother and the dogs got the flock up the hill and left them to graze their way down in their own time. He had recovered six of the sheep that had jumped the broken fence but had found no sign of the seventh. He probably had a long boring job in front of him that day finding the escapee but with the dogs he would do it and preserve his reputation.

There was no telling what a frightened sheep would be likely to do, they were rightly tagged as brainless and would wander helplessly about on familiar ground they had trodden countless times. The dogs knew about finding strays and angled off in different directions when Mannie told them to seek and he kept on a line between them across the face of the sloping grazing towards the trees sweeping up to Rievaulx Moor. It was unlikely the sheep would have gone so far and one of the dogs would chase it up out of some hollow or scattering of rocks.

Twenty minutes later when he was a quarter of a mile from the trees the youngest of the dogs, still a little giddy but learning quickly enough, came out of the trees at a run, barking excitedly. It ran halfway to Mannie, turned about and went again into the wood. Mannie quickened his pace and the old dog came up from the broken ground below.

The young dog, all impatience, kept running in and out of the wood and barking as though telling Mannie to hurry. He had a premonition of what he was going to find and as he went into the gloom of the heavy foliage the feeling of foreboding heightened.

'Tea up!' Alice called from the kitchen door. 'Don't let it get cold.'

Archie was going up the ladder with a stack of slates which he passed to Alan who carried them up the cat ladder to

Pecker. They were doing well and half the roof was reslated. Archie was in the house, Alan at the foot of the ladder and Pecker on the way down when Mannie's old Morris estate car came bumping down the lane. Alan stood leaning on the ladder waiting for him to draw up and before Mannie set the handbrake Alan saw the fleece through the side windows. With an expression that was unreadable he strode slowly across as Mannie opened the rear door and pulled the dead sheep out to the ground, 'First 'un I've ever seen like this an' I've seen some worried sheep.'

The average dog sheep-slayer kills out of ignorant excitement, needlessly except to sate the aroused primitive instinct that proves the early dogs were hunters as well as scavengers. When Mannie turned the carcase on it back and opened the hind legs Alan saw what he meant. The throat had been torn out in the age-old method of slaughter but this sheep's killer had not stopped there. Each side of the fleece-free inner thigh had been stripped of flesh to the bone with just about enough meat taken to make a meal for a ravenous large dog. The cost of one sheep, even on top of all Alan Barnes's losses, was not the end of everything but it is a fact that when a dog has experienced the thrill of killing it becomes addicted. Incurably addicted. And in this case the dog had not killed for fun but apparently out of pure necessity.

'That Lurcher,' Alan ground out flatly, got up off his haunches and shouted, 'Pecker! Pecker! Come an' have a look what that bloody good dog o' yours has done.'

Pecker hurried out with Alice and Archie following. They stood round in a small semi-circle, Mannie still holding the hind legs open.

'Aw, bloody 'ell!' Archie muttered, shaking his head.

Alan directed all his bitterness at Pecker, 'See? See now? If y'd have put a gun to that dog's head instead o' playing stupid games this wouldn't have happened. An' how many more's it goin' to slaughter before we catch it? You ought to be made to pay for 'em all.'

Juttal was the only known stray in that

big area and Pecker conceded to himself that the odds were very heavily in favour of the Lurcher being the culprit, but more than one dog had been wrongly accused of the same crime and until there was conclusive proof that Juttal was guilty Pecker considered him entitled to the same right as humans.

'Hold on a minute, yer seem dead sure it wa' Dempsey. Where'd yer find this sheep, anyroad?'

'In the trees, halfway up from Broadway Foot to the moor,' Mannie told him.

'An' that's where I'm off lookin' for him. Now,' Alan added. 'Come on, Archie, fetch your gun, we'll follow Mannie back to pick his dogs up, they'll sniff the bastard out.'

Alice said practically, 'A few more minutes won't matter and you'll have to have something to eat. I'll go and make some sandwiches.'

Alan threw the sheep into Mannie's car, 'It'll feed the dogs and I'm not hungry.'

'Well I am,' Archie said very definitely, 'I'm not trampin' about all

day on an empty belly. Are you comin',
Pecker?'

Pecker walked to the house with him.
'I might as well, I want to know for sure
if it is Dempsey.' He whistled Nobby in
who had been foraging about the yard,
'Down, stay, there's a job on 'and for
yer.' Nobby dropped flat in the dust.

They ate quickly but not quickly
enough for Alan, with whom the
catching of Juttal had become an
obsession. He chafed when Archie
insisted on drinking all his tea, did not
want to wait the short time it took Alice
to pack food for them to take along.
Pecker reminded him, 'If the dog what
killed the sheep's livin' wild it won't
bother agen till tonight, they onny eat
once a day yer know, yer'll not lose any
more.'

Without replying Alan went out to
start the car.

At Mannie's cottage he had another
chafing wait until Brenda had made tea
for Mannie's vital flask, but eventually
the four armed men with three dogs
started off for Rievaulx Moor. Archie
chatted with Mannie, Alan striding along

in front and Pecker with Nobby at heel in the rear.

They stopped for a breather at the spot where the sheep had been killed and Alan absently touched the brown dried blood coating a tussock with his foot. 'Come on, let's get it over with.' They spread out in a line down the hill, walking slowly, not so much looking for the renegade as trying to find its den. If they could find that, trapping the dog would be easy, though it might well mean a lengthy wait.

The men kept in rough line abreast with the dogs searching in front. The dogs did not know what they were looking for, having been given no sample scent to follow, and even if they had the day-old trail of the killer would quite likely have been too faint. But the dogs could be relied upon to report anything at all unusual, anything that was out of place in their ordered daily lives, and they loved it, accepting it as a game. They dived into thick brush, disappeared into the hollows, came bounding back bright-eyed to be sent off again.

They had been searching more than

two hours when, predictably, it was Nobby who returned to Pecker to bark urgently and dash away up the slope. He transmitted his excitement to the sheepdogs who ran after him and when the men scrambled up to Juttal's overhang they were sniffing about amongst the small rabbit remains. Pecker sighed. The site was a close replica of Juttal's cave on the escarpment, a pointer that he could not turn a blind eye to.

There was all the cover anyone could ask for to set up an ambush and they did it skilfully, spreading out and settling down in thick brush in a rough V to allow Juttal to go right under the overhang, a deployment that also made sure they would not be caught in their own crossfire. There was to be no sentiment or mercy they could not afford, but no unavoidable cruelty, either. When Juttal got home they would all open fire before he had a chance to lie down.

Pecker was at the top of the V to the right of the overhang, the dog would pass closest to him as it came in. He lay propped on his elbows with Nobby at his side, the barrel of the shotgun pushed out in front but yet under cover of the bush. He sensed the wait would be a long one. It was logical if the Lurcher followed the pattern of killer dogs that he would kill and eat again somewhere out on the moors or pastures. Pecker intended the first shot to be his, he meant it to be accurate and at the range of thirty yards knew he could not miss the head and would make the end clean.

Alan was across the overhang from Pecker and Juttal would enter his hole almost sideways on to him, presenting his head as a perfect target. Alan knew he would not miss Archie and Mannie were further down the hill hidden by a tumble of rocks and they would be shooting directly into the hole. There was no chance of Juttal coming out of that trap alive.

The afternoon dragged interminably without cigarettes and they were all willing the sun on its way to the west but at the same time wanting Juttal to come while the light held good enough for shooting. They had torches but the white beams would dazzle them as much as the dog.

Juttal was happy again. The wound had healed over the pellet, the pain gone; there was only the stiffness that reduced his speed but now he did not need his startling acceleration in order to eat. The sheep were much easier to take than rabbit and a far better prize. And that day he did not have to kill again, there was much meat left on the body of his first ovine victim.

He was swinging along from the south-west, homeward bound to come into the woods and his food cache from the south, after a good day of travel, widely skirting villages and farms, staying off the roads. He had been seen by and had seen several men at a distance and when one of them had been in his path he had angled away to the south keeping well clear.

In the warm late evening he passed within a quarter of a mile of a man with two dogs who had shouted and sent him away, but there was no sheep there now. He went in a beeline for the distant wall of trees, swiftly, having found a lope suited his stiff leg better than a trot. He went into the gloom of the wood at the

290

nearest point to his cache and knew he was at the right place although the carcass was gone; the smell would have told him if the bloodstains had not.

He did not search about nor spare one thought to what had happened to the body; the first fact was that it was not there now and the second that he would have to hunt after all. He had not seen any loose grazing sheep for the last three miles or so but he knew there would be some down by the road near the quarry.

Taking, as always, the straightest possible line to his destination he was two hundred yards down the hill below the overhang when he scented the men and dogs. Two men, two dogs. One of the dogs was Nobby, so Pecker would be there too. He stood dead still, sniffing. The men were across the wind a little but their distinctive scent of acrid human sweat was easily readable and Juttal could not fail to distinguish his own kind.

He waited there, letting his nostrils tell him all there was to tell, and sure enough on a stronger puff of wind he picked out the presence of more men. He did not know how many, only that they would not be waiting there to do him any good. He could not get to the overhang without passing close to them and from then on his latest home could be nothing but a place of danger like the cave above the lake. Silently he padded down through the trees in the last of the sun's dappling, making for the quarry. He still had to find food.

The men were more patient than the dogs who had started fretting at such a long period of inactivity when full dark came. The dogs had been very good, reacting willingly to the reminders to stay but the order had to be repeated more and more often and occasionally one would whine its discontent. And one hour after sunset the last of the men's patience ran out. Alan got stiffly to his feet, grunting at the ache in his knees and back. 'Let's get off home, it'd be here by now if it was comin'.'

Disappointed and relieved at the same time they came out of cover, stretching and groaning ruefully. Pecker was no less grateful than Archie and Mannie. He lit a cigarette, deeply inhaled the first lungful of smoke but said as he exhaled, 'This is where 'e lives, I still reckon 'e'll come.'

Archie said, 'Well you can stay if yer like, I've 'ad enough for one night.'

'And me,' Mannie endorsed, stamping the life back into his right foot.

Alan broke his gun and unloaded, 'If that dog's as sly as Lurchers are supposed to be I wouldn't be surprised if it'd twigged us, it might be sittin' up there waitin' for us to go.'

Pecker contradicted, 'No, they 'aven't the brains for that an' Lurchers don't think any different to other dogs. If 'e did wind us 'e'll be well away by now an' I reckon that's what 'appened.' Venting their various theories they called the dogs in from wetting the tree trunks and started the hike back to the cars.

Early the morning after the news flashed from farm to farm by telephone, reaching Lane End in the middle of breakfast. A lamb had been killed and partly eaten not far from the hamlet of Laskill which straddled the Seph a mile and a quarter above the fork. The killer had not been sighted.

Through the eyes of a hillfarmer the situation had reached a stage of emergency. No flock could be counted as safe while the outlaw was at large, every shepherd carried his gun and firearms went into car boots and dangled from jolting tractor seats. Stricter watch was kept on the flocks and the shepherds stayed with them on grazing that had always been safe.

And Juttal became famous or infamous according to whether a man was a sheep farmer or fireside reader of newspapers. With not much happening in Parliament and the close season football transfer market unusually quiet the local Press seized on the saga of the 'four-legged pirate' as a welcome space-filler. The national dailies and giant Sunday newspapers took the lead from their provincial colleagues and unknowledgeable journalists made the common mistakes. One renowned columnist had it that Juttal was outwitting his hunters, another that the dog was taking some kind of revenge. He was described as a ghost dog, a wraith, a canine commando who came from nowhere and vanished into the ground after a raid. He did not get the same billing as Malcolm Macdonald or Kerry Packer but for two weeks there was hardly an edition that did not give him a mention. And true to his contrary nature the man in the street developed a sneaking liking for the dog that was 'showing all them farmers the way home'. One wealthy crank who professed to be an animal lover offered a substantial reward to the man who could deliver Juttal alive to his baronial home.

Juttal, unaware that he was causing any disturbance at all, simply got on with his life as his instinct and circumstances dictated. He had a whole world to roam in, water to drink, food to eat and to a dog enough is sufficient—except on the odd occasion when he would gorge until he was sick.

One point which baffled the experts was his eating habit. He did not kill every day, the dead sheep he left behind were always removed by the owners and therefore it was assumed he did not eat every day as a normal dog would. But what the experts could not know was that Juttal had regained his speed and when dinnertime came around he would catch and eat the animal which happened to be handiest. He had *not* turned into a compulsive sheep slaughterer and sometimes, if he was not feeling too hungry, would pass sheep over for the heady thrill of bringing down a hurtling rabbit or hare.

Another puzzling point, especially to Pecker Johnson, was that Juttal did not appear to be living to a pattern as a dog is expected to. Until the abortive attempt to shoot him down Pecker had been able to whittle down the area in which Juttal was living to the vicinity of Rievaulx Moor. Now the reported sightings told him nothing. One day he would be seen on Hutton ridge, the next Danby Low Moor, then Glaisdale Moor on the day before he was seen running into the sunset carrying a fluttering cockerel from a farm near Ugthorpe. There were not many of the 553 square miles of that national park Juttal did not see and if he had not come to hate man actively he had certainly no cause to seek out his company. Therefore, whenever possible, Juttal kept to the high ground, the higher the better for man seemed to be a creature of the valleys for preference.

At first the farmers were the only ones actually wishing him dead and then he made a mortal enemy of another body of men, a zealous and jealous organisation, the National Parks Commission.

It had been a day of heavy rain, one of those surprising downpours that come with almost no warning and make Britain one of the greenest countries in the world. It had been noisy in the woods as it is when the sheeting cloudburst hammers into thick foliage and to Juttal that kind of weather precipitated thunder. It did not thunder but he nevertheless played safe by lying up all day close to the knobbly bole of an old oak. And because there was nothing to occupy his mind he slept most of the time, so that when the rain stopped in the first dark hour he was wide awake, full of running and very hungry.

Prospects of finding a meal at that hour were not good. He could scent and even see prey in the dark but catching it was another matter and he moved off to the south after hearing an inviting rustling from that direction. Like the ghost he had been labelled, his pale shape threaded through the trees in the increasing starlight. Whatever had made the rustling had gone when he got to the thick brush and simply because he was already going that way he carried on southward.

For three miles he trotted on with the ground imperceptibly dropping lower and lower, farther south than he had been since becoming an outlaw, where the small thick copses and woods were more numerous and the farms closer together.

He stopped to urinate before entering an extensive stand of trees and was having a shake when the breeze brought him the scent. It was the scent of food he knew, but what food he did not. It was not his first experience of this scent but he had never seen the animal that made it, it was as unlike sheep, rabbit or hare as was the strong-smelling fox, but much more enticing than any fox. Quietly he went round a dense clump of bushes, following the breeze-wafted trail.

Fifty yards he moved cautiously into the dark trees, getting closer all the time, keen eyes stabbing and flicking right and left and he was nearly on top of them before their nerve gave way and they broke cover, several dark bodies bigger than himself springing up and crashing away to the south. With a victorious snarl of anticipation he went after them with such force from a standing start that his pedigree father would not have been ashamed of him.

Juttal had never thrilled to such a chase as this and only lifelong habit kept him from barking his joy. The animals could run and jump, too, and twist and turn around the black trunks without a break in their stride, and were all but a match for the dog skidding after them. Not quite a match, though, and he steadily gained on the back marker, a smaller beast than its companions.

They burst out of the trees on to a long, wide straight expanse of short grass. Twenty yards away the antlered leader of the herd was galloping for the wall of trees across the clearing but

Juttal's hungering fangs were now level with the fawn's rump. Out of the trees, the domain of the deer, and on to grassland where legs could be stretched Juttal moved easily along the fawn's flank and came up under the throat as the fawn tried to turn away from him. Locked in the death hold they somersaulted, writhed a few moments in a struggle that could not have been called a fight. Then Juttal got up to decide how best the kill could be eaten. As he sniffed along the warm body the crashing of the herd faded, and finally stopped when it took fresh cover for the night, the buck judging it was safe again.

Juttal found this was a good kind of food with no fur, fleece or feathers to remove. He ate his fill of the tender haunch and went back under the nearest trees to sleep.

He had been fortunate in walking practically on top of the herd. If he had passed a few yards to the right or left the shyest of all wild animals would have waited it out and let him pass, which he might have done, in bafflement when the scent vanished. By force of circumstances deer have become very adept at staying out of sight. Hunted for centuries by man and beast they are timid and suspicious to the extreme, knowing how to blend in with their woodland home and even the stag's antlers, the herd's only weapon, have evolved in the shape of small branches.

The deer on national parkland are protected animals, given encouragement and protection to breed by dedicated wardens who frown severely on poachers of any kind, and in the mid morning when the body of the fawn was found a search was made at once for the killer. Juttal's scent was picked up and followed by an old and skilful tracking dog. To the north they trailed, to where the high moors started to rise, where on that clear day a man could literally see for miles. When they could not sight the big yellow dog they blamed, they turned around to go back to the disturbed peace of their woodlands.

# CHAPTER 10

The average countryman owes the greater part of his livelihood to the quality of patience, watching his capital slowly increase or shrink as his cattle and crops flourish or wilt. He extends this patience to the other aspects of his life and rarely gets into the tearing hurries that are the daily experiences of city folk. And even when he decides that speed is desirable he is not, so to speak, fast out of the trap.

The entire population of the North Yorkshire Moors was by this time up in arms about Juttal's outrages and the people who lived in the part where Juttal had made his homes were also furious with themselves over their failure to run him down. It was with a large-scale hunt in mind that a meeting was called with an open invitation to all concerned. For more reasons than one the interested parties were asked to assemble in the tap room of the Spotted Dog.

On the morning of the day of the meeting Jim McConnachie went quickly through the pages of the *Mail* as Paula poured his second cup of tea.

'Mm,' he said, 'they've given him a miss today.'

'Who?'

'The Lurcher.'

'Are you going?'

'To the meeting? Yes, I think so.'

Paula put down her cup, 'You don't have to. It's really not your business. You've enough to do without volunteering for anything else.'

He smiled, 'I suppose I'm being nosey, really, but there's something about that dog—'

The telephone rang and when he went out into the hall the dogs crowded with him, knowing the ringing bell could mean a sudden departure on an emergency call. When he picked up the receiver, Fred scowled. Rufus grinned.

'Jim McConnachie here.'

'Good morning, Yorkshire Television, Roger Greenwood calling, I'll put you through,' the telephonist sing-songed and after the clicking Jim smiled at the honest Lancashire voice asking him if he was well. He had been interviewed twice in the past and had watched himself after tea on the local magazine programme, *Calendar*. With the greetings and platitudes out of the way Roger told him, 'We want to do a film about this killer dog you've got running loose up there and we thought you might give us a bit of help.'

'Glad to if I can,' Jim grinned, not at all displeased at the thought of working with a film crew again, 'but you'll have to be quick, the farmers are meeting tonight to organise a big hunt for the dog. I'll be surprised if he's still loose after tomorrow.'

'You've seen the dog, haven't you? Is it really a super dog or something? I mean according to reports it can give everyone the runaround.'

'Och no, don't believe that stuff. It's a fast dog that knows how to live off the country but it was partly trained for that by the old gipsy who died and left it stranded up here. And I'll tell you something else, it's not a bad 'un all it's doing is trying to stay alive and you can't blame anyone or anything for that, now can you?'

'Certainly not, Mr McConnachie, but this one's caught the public's imagination and you'll have seen some of the things in the papers. Anyway, you say the farmers will be out in force in the morning so we'll have to get a crew up there bright and early—d'you think the farmers would object if I came up to the meeting?'

'They can't there's an open invitation and anyway they're holding it in a local pub and the landlord'll see no one gets refused. The Spotted Dog, eight o'clock sharp.'

'Thanks very much and I won't waste any more of your time. See you at the meeting?'

The dogs preceded Jim back into the dining room and took up their stations on the hearth rug. Paula rubbed toast crumbs from her finger tips, 'Are we going to be a telly star again?' she teased him.

'Superstar,' was the only retort he

could think of. He finished his tea and the dogs led him out to the car to start the morning round.

Basically a shy man who liked privacy Jim had only agreed to broadcast to help people understand consequences during the rabies scare, to emphasise the stupidity of smuggling animals into the country however beloved those pets might be, and once again in a documentary about the National Park and the prime necessity of visitors leaving the countryside as they found it. He still had his leg pulled about it.

The tenant of the Spotted Dog was sweating and quite happy to be so. It was five minutes past eight and his taproom was packed to the doors. Alan Barnes was waiting to open the meeting until the last two arrivals, Jim and Roger Greenwood, had been served. When the till slammed shut on their money he stood up and the general chatter died away.

'Everybody knows why we're here so we can get straight down to it. Who's got any ideas about catchin' this bloody dog.'

There were plenty of ideas, all of which would have worked had Juttal been accommodating enough to do the things expected of him, but with his being so unpredictable each suggestion was cried down. Alan, who had given more thought to the problem than anyone else, let each man have his say before putting his own proposal.

'Seeing as this dog doesn't seem to live anywhere special we'll have to rely on catching sight of him early in the morning and then we'll have to act fast, drop whatever we're doing and get him bottled up so tight he can't get away. There's enough of us.'

'That's all right, he gets sighted often enough but he'd be miles away by the time we all got there. He doesn't hang about, y'know.' The speaker was a dour, stocky man who farmed to the north of Rievaulx Moor and had lost two lambs to Juttal.

'Take it from me, one sighting's all we need provided the weather's good and I'll tell you how we'll do it.' Alan knew his plan was a good one and like most workable schemes it was simple to him. It

307

did not appear so to many of the others, especially the older men, but he replied to their objections simply and shortly and, as no one else came up with anything offering the same chance of success, when he put it to the vote there were no dissenters.

Roger took a good swallow of his drink and held it up to the light. 'Very morish is this, I'll have to watch it, I've a long drive home.' He glanced round the room at the weathered faces. 'One thing, these blokes don't mess about when they decide to act.'

'Aye, it takes a lot to rouse them —they've got to be able to take setbacks in their business—but when they do get vexed...'

After fixing up communications arrangements with Jim, the television personality wisely drank up and went home. Pecker Johnson, who had not contributed one word to the discussion, also drained his glass and went to have it refilled.

After a mass exchange of telephone numbers, and aided by the beer, the atmosphere changed to a happier one.

Before the barman called time, everyone was so sure Alan's plan would succeed that Juttal was already looked upon as dead.

**\* \* \* \***

Alan Barnes was sitting in the office of the gliding club. They had not turned on the lights and he could just make out the shape of Stanley Marsden in the first grey creeping of the false dawn. Outside already warmed up was the Piper Cub, the weapon on which Alan's plan depended.

This was the third morning after the meeting and the first fine one with the required weather conditions. He had risen early on the two preceding days only to get back into bed on seeing the rain and clouds from the window. At that moment across the wide scattering of farms men would be climbing to high vantage points, most with binoculars and all with guns. If the dog showed itself anywhere in the western half of the park—where it was most likely to—it would be in the trap and killed within an hour. Alan felt like talking and wished Stanley, who was snoring softly in his chair, would wake up.

He watched the grey morning lighten and brighten, listened to the first songs of the awakening birds, thought about his promise to Joan and thought that at least his life would be settled one way or the other by the same time the following year. Since he had promised they would marry Joan had not missed any opportunity to raise the subject, and as she had forecast, her daughter Barbara had been delighted, impishly demanding to have a say in the naming of their first born and earning herself a not entirely angry scolding from her mother.

Finally, sick of his own mental conversation he reached out to pick up the kettle and selfishly rattle it to wake Stanley when, with a preliminary ting, the telephone shrilled. Stanley woke with a jerk and nearly fell from his chair, Alan snatched up the receiver.

With a chain reaction, as each person alerted telephoned another, the western half of the North Yorkshire Moors came to life and went to work.

Juttal woke when the first light of the sun struck his eyelids. He had slept, as he often did now, at the base of a tree and the first thing he wanted was a drink. He came from under the trees and crossed the open grazing land, heading down the hill to where a little stream cut through the heather. A half mile away a man thrust his field glasses back into the case and he also ran down a hill, back to his farm and telephone. After making the call he ran out again, this time with only his gun, and he was panting heavily when he got to the place he had seen Juttal. But Juttal had gone. The man turned and ran again, again back to the farm where he drove his Land-Rover out of the barn and left the engine running as he shaded his eyes to search the sky to the south west. He saw the little aircraft long before he heard the engine, knowing that many more pairs of eyes would be watching its progress, waiting for the signal to converge.

Juttal, oblivious of these elaborate preparations to kill him, ambled along in a southerly direction, playing at chasing the gulls into the air. The heavy white birds could only scream in anger at him for disturbing them. Playfully he chased thrushes, pheasants, blackbirds, anything he saw that he could send flapping away in fear, but because he was not hungry he was not serious about the chases, it was just something to do. Keeping to the highest ground available he did not have to go out of his way to avoid men, and even though he heard the drone of the low-flying aircraft it meant nothing to him. He had heard and seen many of them and they had never hurt him.

Stanley Marsden flew directly to the point he had marked on the reference grid of the map. In the passenger seat Alan was sitting with the binoculars at the ready, staring out over the nose. Four miles from his own farm he knew exactly the spot where the dog had been seen, and against the grey-green of the moorland its yellow coat should stand out clearly. Alan pointed ahead and slightly to starboard. Stanley nodded, altered course a fraction, and when Alan touched his shoulder he banked and turned into a wide circle.

In sharp relief, in the bright light and deep-etched shadows, the ground below stood out three dimensionally: the rolling hills and strips and clumps of woodlands. Alan touched Stanley's shoulder again, jabbing down with a finger. Stanley adjusted the controls and they began a shallow spiralling descent.

When Pecker Johnson had been given Juttal's position a picture of the surrounding terrain had jumped immediately into his mind. Every volunteer on the hunt knew his own land intimately, every rock and cranny, stream and tree, everyone also knew the now designated hunting ground fairly well. But none of them had the comprehensive knowledge of the country that Pecker had, had to have to ply his illicit trade. He could not use maps and compasses, had no idea how to navigate by technical means, but as he put the grimy receiver back on the dusty cradle he knew exactly which route he was going to take. He believed that because he knew dogs, had made allowances for Juttal's uncharacteristic behaviour and an educated guess at what the dog would do in the circumstances, it

313

was about to find itself. He knew he needed lots of luck and that luck is something that cannot be willed or coaxed.

He held the van door open for Nobby to jump in and, as he braked at his gate before driving out onto the road, Jim McConnachie drove by followed by a Range-Rover marked with the sign of Yorkshire Television. He stayed behind them up Sutton Bank and for six miles into the narrow snaking B-class roads leading to the moor, then he turned off to climb a steep track he should not have asked of his vehicle, but careful nursing got him to the top of the hill where he wanted to be. Slinging the binoculars on his shoulder, he hurried to a twenty-foot heap of black rocks, climbed to the summit, sat down and fastened his eyes on the circling aircraft. He had not been in position long when the wings waggled, waggled again, and the pilot tightened the circle. They had pinpointed Juttal and they would fly the circle above him as the hunters closed in. Pecker watched intently, nodded and grinned at his accurate guesswork as, quite plainly, with each revolution the Piper Cub was coming closer to him.

Below his rocky lookout post a hundred yards down the slope a narrow belt of trees ran east and west. Beyond that was a mile or so of tableland bare of anything but heather, bracken and ferns. He scrambled down the rocks back to the van, he would have to be quick and still needed an awful lot of luck but if he got that luck he knew it would work. He started the engine and bumped across the grass to get under the cover of the trees.

From the roads to the east and west, from the farms to the north, armed men hurried upward, those on the southern tips of the two prongs running, where the ground allowed, to close the gap and seal the dog in the trap, glancing up from time to time to check the circling course of the aircraft.

Juttal climbed a steep, rocky slope and came up on to the flat moor that shelved gently down to the line of trees in the south. When the aircraft roared across in front of him he paused a moment to follow its flight and saw, on his flank, the head of a man appear over the sharp skyline. The head was no more than a dot in the distance, but instantly recognisable for what it was, and when Juttal moved off again it was at his fast travelling lope, his long body stretching and bunching with the effortless grace of his father. He heard a shout answered by another and then the aircraft thundered across his path again. All this unexpected activity set his nerves singing, his defence mechanism working. His defence against man was his speed. His haunches thrust, his forelegs reached out, and as though he were chasing a hare he streaked at full gallop along the centre of the plateau.

Men were coming into his view all along both skylines now, shouting, running men, but there were none to the south and soon he had passed the last of them and the shelter of the trees was only a quarter of a mile away, a few seconds for him.

He was nearly there when a man came out of the trees to his right, Juttal saw it was Pecker but that did not matter, he swerved a little to his left, driving for the trees when the gun banged and there was a rattling swoosh in the foliage over his head. He ran on for ten yards into the trees before he was stopped abruptly, bowled over, gripped inextricably in the folds of a loosely-spread net. He struggled, even more so when Pecker came up with Nobby to wrap the net even tighter around him, and only lay still in defeat when Pecker told Nobby to heel and ran off again.

They were all up on the plateau by then, more than thirty men all running to where Pecker had gone into the trees, running in a ragged stream of varying speeds as age permitted. Pecker came out into the open, swung an arm to the east and started to run in that direction. The aircraft had been coming in on a low curve, it altered course to pass over Pecker's head and followed the tree line where it went over the ridge to merge with the woods on the slope. Pecker tripped and fell, cursing, yelling at everyone for greater effort or the dog was going to escape again. He sat rubbing his ankle until the last man had gone by, then he got up and went quickly back to where he had left Juttal.

Nobby was there before him, having a sniff at his former colleague, with Juttal glaring balefully out through the meshes. Pecker had no time for niceties, he went the twenty yards to the van, opened the rear doors and put his gun inside. He went back, took two handfuls of loose net and unceremoniously dragged the squirming Juttal over the rough ground. With a grunting heave he swung the dog bodily, net and all, into the van, slammed the doors and drove away as fast as he dared on that surface. From the road he caught sight of the Piper again as it turned from one of its sweeps and disappeared to the east.

George Thurnscoe tossed his head in annoyance, got up out of his chair, went to the open door of the caravan and shouted:

'Quiet you lot, I'm tryin' to watch the bleedin' telly.' The noise level made by the playing children dropped and George went back inside knowing the peace would not last very long.

The trailer caravan was luxurious, his wife came from the kitchenette with a blue-striped pint pot of strong tea, ''Ere y'are, love, don't let it get cold.'

He grunted as he blindly took the tea, eyes glued again to the shapely girl dancers.

Not for George and family the traditional deprivations of living on the road. A widely-known dealer in scrap metal, his long and industrious working day was bringing him reasonable wealth and his home on wheels had every modern appointment devised by the caravan's designer. Grouped around George's caravan on the waste ground were seven others intermingled with an assortment of lorries, vans and cars most of which belonged to George.

The squad of children, followed by the noisy dog pack, screamed and yelled as they ran round under and over the vehicles and again broke his concentration on the undulating limbs. George gave best to the exuberance of childhood.

'Bloody doylems,' he said.

His wife, the daughter of another prominent gipsy family laughed. 'Keep you 'air on, chava.'

The old Romany language of their parents was gradually falling into disuse, although they made their English more colourful by injecting the odd word.

The yelling of the children had faded to the far end of the waste ground and now it came closer again until they were clamouring right outside his door. Scowling at his laughing wife he heaved himself up, flung open the door to shout for quiet when he saw the cause of the disturbance was a tall, thin stranger who was pushing through the gang.

'Can I 'ave a word wi' yer?' Pecker shouted.

'What about?' George asked suspiciously.

Pecker looked helplessly at the milling children and George descended the two steps to lightly cuff a few ears and drive them away.

'Nah then,' he invited bluntly, ungraciously. Strangers on camp sites often meant eviction notices or probing queries from Inland Revenue officials.

Pecker lit a cigarette and flicked away the match. 'I'm tryin' to find someone 'oo knew an old gipsy 'oo snuffed it a few weeks ago up above Thirsk.'

'Albert Lee? Yer've found someone, then, 'e was my cousin. What can I do for yer?'

Pecker grinned, 'Ah've got some of 'is property.'

George grinned, 'Oh, aye, what is it?'

'Can we to inside an' talk a minute first?'

George held open the door for him.

The commercial stressing the vital need for ladies to smear their faces daily with a sickly-looking oily jelly flashed off the screen and the strident five-note fanfare heralded the second part of *Calendar,* Marylyn Webb smiled: 'Welcome back. Now for more news about the wild dog. Roger Greenwood and the camera crew were up very early this morning to film the organised hunt and here's the result of their efforts...'

The film was unsteady, taken hurriedly with the camara hand held and showed Juttal racing toward the trees, Pecker coming into view, taking aim and firing, and Juttal disappearing into the deep shadow. Pecker ran in after him, came out a few seconds later and redirected the running men. There were shots of the Piper Cub and the farmers streaming away to the east, when Pecker walking away in the opposite direction. The screen blanked for an instant and the pretty blonde reappeared. 'And that was that. The dog hasn't been seen since but the farmers are determined to catch it...'

'You know,' Jim McConnachie said to Paula, 'Pecker didn't try to hit that Lurcher, he couldn't have missed at that range, and did you notice he wasn't limping at all when he walked away.'

'What do you mean?'

Jim smiled slowly. 'I don't know, to be honest, but that Pecker's so devious you never can tell with him. I've a feeling we've seen the last of that dog. I hope so, anyway.'

'You can't think he'd try to keep it!'

Jim shook his head, 'He couldn't do that. I don't know what he's up to but I think this episode's going to have a happier ending than I imagined.'

It was warm lying in the dust on the sunny side of the caravan watching the children play and the other dogs roam about. Juttal could not roam about like them, he had a certain amount of freedom to the extent of the long chain tied to the stake driven deeply into the ground. He was not unhappy now.

At first he had fretted for his liberty, for days he had pulled at the chain, longed to get out of this city and back to his own world but gradually, with his practical fatalism, he had started to accept this new life. He was treated kindly, fed well and he could understand some of the things said to him and whenever he was praised with 'cushty juttal' his tail would wag.

With a fixed abode the old protectiveness came back and the other dogs soon learned the folly of encroaching on his territory which was exactly the length of the chain. He had not attempted to harm any of the children but they did not fully trust him and played their games well out of his reach.

The two young Thurnscoes soon made friends with him, for it was usually one of George's sons who came out to feed him and they were proud to own the best fighting dog on the road. As for George, it was well worth the cost of Juttal's keep to be able to teleview with the noise of the children kept in the background. A dog man born and bred, he quickly saw Juttal's many good points. He would never again have the slightest qualm about the safety of his hoard of five-pound notes hidden in the caravan. He promised himself that if ever he met Pecker again he would buy him all the beer he could drink at a sitting.

George woke from his after-dinner nap, yawned loudly and stretched mightily. 'I'll just take the dog out before I go for a pint. Get yourself ready if you want to come,' he said to his wife.

Juttal was waiting at the door for him, standing patiently to have the chain replaced by the piece of rope that served as a lead and went willingly to enjoy the highlight of his day.